Cripples & Creeps

stories and a poem

Jude Davison

Also by Jude Davison

BOOKS

Uncertain Heaven
Cybersoul
The Underwater Birds
A Writer's Prerogative
Small cruelties - stories

ALBUMS

Back to the Wonderful
Strange Fruit
Neurotic Erotica
God's Big Radio
Angels in the Slipstream
Blue Martian Dusk
Lizard Man
Highway Blues
Ordinary Dream
Bread & Bones
Circo de Teatro
Outskirts of Eden
Head Bone Gumbo
Cybersoul

Cripples & Creeps

stories and a poem

Copyright © 2016 Jude Davison

www.judedavison.co.uk

All rights reserved. This book is copyright material and must not be copied, reproduced, transferred, distributed. Leased, licensed or publicly performed or used in any way except as specifically permitted in writing by the publisher, as allowed under the terms and conditions under which it was purchased or as strictly permitted by applicable copyright law. Any unauthorized distribution or use of this text may be a direct infringement of the author's and publisher's rights, and those responsible may be liable in law accordingly.

ISBN: 9798332246173

Cover Design & Artwork: Jude Davison
Cover art photo – Eric Vondy
Published by Pigeon Moods Music
www.judedavison.co.uk

For Thea

Contents

Stories

1. The Bible Seller

22. Turner

43. Love Locks

60. Hope

85. Waiting for God

101. Bruce Lee Fatal Roundhouse Kick

118. Disappearing man

155. Sticks & Stones

167. Miss Information

183. Luck

A Poem

214. Cripples & Creeps

The Bible Seller

The Bible seller had always plied his trade the old-fashioned way - selling his wares door-to-door. He carried a large case that contained all his pamphlets and samples. It is hard to think that there could be so many different variations of one product. But there was. There was a wide range of Bibles, some for the more budget minded and others for those who could afford, and who desired, the top-of-the-line leather-bound limited edition or massive family heirloom types. Versions which collected, in great opulence, the most celebrated writings in the Christian world and were destined to be handed down from generation to generation. But he also carried standard paperbacks, and some with illustrations: Jesus holding a lamb, Moses parting the Red Sea, Noah building his ark. He had large print books, pocketbooks, audio-book versions that came in a ten CD box set read by soothing-voiced narrators like Solomon Burke. The Old Testament and the New, there was a version for everyone. He hadn't always sold Bibles; he'd started out as a vacuum cleaner salesman. But he quickly found that selling practical things had its drawbacks. All those moving parts, all the things that could go wrong. Plus, there was the warranties, repairs, returns to deal with. No, the profit margin in Bibles was better and returns were almost non-existent. It seemed that no-one ever wanted a refund on the word of God.

The Bible seller began another day's work in a new area of town. The streets here were quiet, residential. He had a well-worn banter he used, but what salesman worthy of their salt didn't? But he prided himself on not being too pushy, too salesman-like. His approach was more like a friend come to do you a favour or return something you'd lost or forgotten. He once calculated that the average time he took with each client was forty-eight minutes. From his opening preamble to closing the deal and issuing a receipt, forty-eight minutes was a decent enough time. Enough time for people to get a good sense of him. Trust him. He also calculated that at that rate he could sell 8.75 Bibles a day, naturally calculating in an hour for his lunch break. But what he actually averaged was four or five. Sometimes he did better, when he sold multiple sets in one sale - gifts for family and friends. But that was more unusual than the norm. No, four or five a day was a satisfyingly average quota. People warmed to his non-rushed manner, his friendly and pleasant demeanour. He would often be offered a cup of tea and sometimes cake or biscuits, people knew they could trust a man who sold Bibles for his livelihood. The Bible seller was a world apart from those other salesmen, the ones who sold cars on Eddie's Used Car Lot.

Eddie's stood on the outskirts of town, at the end of the end of a seemingly endless strip-mall. Past the burger joints and pizza shops, the Mexican and Chinese all-you-can-eat-buffet restaurants, the Factory Carpet Outlets, Furniture Jungles, Toys R Us, and Bride's-Wear Emporiums. Past discount jewellers, pet food megastores, stores that went by names such as Guns 'n Gold, Big Al's Army Surplus, and the Computer One-Stop Direct. And not to mention the stand-alone giants - Sears and Walmart. Places you can only get to by car. With vast parking lots of cracked concrete and asphalt that heated up and softened in the height of the late afternoon sun. That two-hour stretch of summer day when everything reached its apex. The heat, the glare that became murderous, unbearable. When nothing moved. No-one ventured outside. The air was still, suffocating and oppressive. Everyone retreated to the air-conditioned comfort of the shopping malls, diners, bowling alleys and darkened barrooms to wait it out until the cool of evening when people would return to the streets once again.
Eddie's attracted all sorts of clientele, but mostly people looking for a cheap deal. A set of wheels at a budget price.

The trick was all in the word reliable. That's what got folk's attention. Top of the list - a reliable ride. Second was air-conditioning - the first thing to go on a used car. 'She runs like a dream - but the air-con is a little subtle'. But something people would gamely overlook if the vehicle was deemed to be otherwise reliable. The wish lists could be extensive though, and not to mention hopeful - leather upholstery, saloon, station-wagon, medium compact, hatchback, standard transmission, automatic, convertible, four-door, two-door, you name it. A fancy ride at a no-frills price - but everything paled against reliability. The guys at Eddie's were slick as foxes and wily as weasels and took no prisoners when it came to hammering out a deal. Fast with the tongue, quick with numbers, and knowing how to spot a sucker were the only pre-requisites needed to sell cars at Eddie's.

Next door to Eddie's, the last place on the strip was a road house named 'Abe's Wild West'. Which technically placed it on the edge of town. That mythical place - the edge of town, like some sort of no-man's land. A twilight zone of unreality that seemed to exist in its own vacuum of time and space. Which seemed like a fitting place to find a strip joint. With no windows it was dark on the inside and it had a cheap neon sign that always had a least one letter burnt out. The outside was plainly stuccoed, so Abe's Wild West didn't look remarkable or draw attention to itself. Seven nights a week, around eight o'clock, right after happy hour, the girls would hit the stage. From 8:00pm to 2:00am there would be a near constant parade of strippers entertaining the tattooed furry-armed men who drove to Abe's in their pickup trucks, Harley's, and Camaro's. By nine the parking lot would be full and by then there was bound to have already been at least one fight out there. Nothing fatal just old-fashioned punch-ups by frustrated testosterone-fuelled men burning off a little post-work steam pumped up on too many rum 'n cokes, heavy metal, and untouchable naked women who spread their womanly glory right in your face, yet so far out of reach.

The women preferred to call themselves dancers. It added a subtle upgrade to their trade. They danced three songs each set: two on the pole and one on the floor. They worked one set each hour and filled the gaps by table-dancing. Ten bucks got you five horny minutes with tits close enough you could smell them. A heady mixture of stale perfume, sweat and cigarette smoke. Every girl smelled the same - stripper's cologne. And every girl had that detached faraway look in her eyes. They stripped at their own pace, taking their time to get down to the final gynaecological reveal. The waxed and shaved nether regions. But the dancers had to be fully naked by the third and final song. Club rules. It's what brought the hirsute hoards back for more. Abe's was known for its 'full nudity', no G-string shows. Not every club could boast that. But the edge of town was indeed the Wild West; it made its own rules. The girls got to choose their own music, spun by the resident DJ who pumped up the crowd, intro'd each dancer, and advertised the bar's nightly specials: two-for-one shots, sleazy-named shooters like 'sex on the beach', 'blow-jobs', and cheap jugs of Coors. The music was inevitably plucked from the eighties hair-metal catalogues of bands like Poison, Bon Jovi, Guns 'n Roses or Van Halen, typically some rock ballad by the time they hit the rug for the floor-show. A fun-fur mat about two-metre square spread out on the stage for the girls to get down and express their more artistic moves or simply simulate fantasy sexual positions. One dancer that out-shined all the rest on the rug was Florence. Flo was tough as nails, hailed from Montreal, used the stage name Candy Floss, and had a prosthetic leg that came off at the knee.

Danny had worked at Eddie's for five years. In that time he'd worked his way up from car washer to sales. He was voted salesman of the month on twelve separate occasions. On casual Fridays he never dressed down. He believed that you never get a second chance to make a first impression. His Friday sales eclipsed everyone else's. He knew lots of people but had no real friends. He could read a room like others read a book, his instincts were deadly accurate and he always said he could smell money. After work on Fridays he would stop off for a burger at Randy's Diner and then head to Abe's for a few beers. He mostly went there because he knew that a lone wolf could always blend in at Abe's - strip clubs weren't pack animal domains, they were the territory of the single guy or horny husbands getting a close up look at what their wives would never reveal quite so blatantly. Danny watched the strippers work the room like he scoped-out losers checking out cars on the lot. It was the same old story. The devil is in the details. Everyone reveals more than they realise. He could tell which girls were high on dope and which ones gave blow jobs for a little extra money on the side. Which ones were clean and which ones would give you a dose of the clap. He was fascinated by Flo. He liked her floor show the best. She would do things none of the other girls could even come close to. She was seductive and would make eye contact with the customers with her smoky dark eyes, and draw them in. She didn't try to hide the fact that she had a fake leg, in fact she celebrated it. She had hand-painted it with Asian symbols, a skull and crossbones motif and her name in stylised pink and black lettering. Her most infamous trick involved ping pong balls. Once down on the rug she would take off her leg, put a ping pong ball into her snatch and while lying on her back she would shoot it up into the air. Then she would use her prosthetic limb and stump to volley it back and forth like David Beckham doing drills. It was fascinating to watch. She never missed. If Abe's had a stripper of the month award she would have owned it. To finish her act she would shoot another ping pong ball straight at one lucky customer. Someone she'd singled out. A souvenir from Candy Floss. Danny had three of her balls. He kept every one. He valued the fact she went the extra mile and developed her act into a proper show - a little razzmatazz. It reminded him of closing the deal on the lot. The big finale. Danny always said it was more about the sizzle than the steak.

In his spare time the Bible seller loved to read. His latest thing was crime novels. He liked the psychological thrillers the best. His current interest was in psychopaths. Once he got interested in something he would absorb it, immerse himself in it, study it from every angle. He had exhausted many different subject areas already. From Polynesian antiquity, to mammals of Australasia, to religions of the world, he drank it all up. That's how he got into the Bible business - through religious studies. He hadn't been raised by a God-fearing family, fact was, he didn't have a real family at all. He grew up in an orphanage for boys, the nearest he got to knowing God was in the simple prayers offered up by the Brothers before mealtimes.

'For what we are about to receive - Amen'. Giving thanks for the simple things in life. He had a longing to feel something deeper though, to truly understand this love of God. He'd watch the Brothers with an intense curiosity as they went about their daily prayers and errands. But the Brothers went about their Godly business with a solemn intent. Theirs was a need to serve, not to promote. They had no interest in the longing of a young boy's desires.

St. Cross Home for Boys was solemn and spartan institute. There was no love to be found in the cold concrete halls. These institutions served a purpose alright, filled a need, and in many ways were the plain measure of good in a civilised society. Meeting the basic human needs. How we treat our downtrodden, sick, homeless, and criminals is an indication of the very fabric of the values in which we build our society. Pro-life or pro-choice? Death penalty or mercy? God-fearing or agnostic? Simple choices which define us. Life in an institution would come to define the Bible seller. He carried his empty sadness with him for years until one day he got an answer to his prayers. He came across a discarded pamphlet that told of a glorious land, a future guaranteed, a life like none-other. There were places to be had in this Promised Land. There was a place set aside for him if he wanted it. All he had to do was accept the Word. Who could resist? So he made his promise to God, then he did what he always had, he immersed himself into the world's religions with a passion and a curiosity that would have been worthy of a doctorate. He wanted to be sure he had the right God, had made the right choice. From Islam to Paganism, Tao to Buddhism he read everything he could get his hands on. Gods that had been worshipped since the dawn of time. Benevolent rulers. Deities found in the sun and stars, their images depicted on crumbling ancient tombs. Merciful Gods, revengeful ones full of promise and fear. He explored it all. At the heart of every great religion was a charismatic leader who could conjure magic, someone who dealt in miracles. In many ways there was a great similarity to the serial killers he was currently reading about. Ted Bundy and Jesus Christ, they shared the same charm and magnetism. They had brilliant minds and were both great manipulators in their own way. The Bible seller was always fascinated by how minds worked, what made them tick. One thing that he found most intriguing was the fact that psychopaths never dream.

Danny liked to shoot his BB gun in the woods. It was his weekend hobby. Besides closing the deal with some sucker, it was the only thing he got excited about. He would shoot at anything and everything: tin cans, fence posts, beer bottles, animals and birds. He didn't feel guilty about shooting living things; he didn't have a conscience about killing. As a boy he used to catch insects, bugs, butterflies, whatever was around, he calmly, and without remorse, would mutilate them one at a time. Delicately and artistically he would create a circus of crippled animals. Ants with no legs. A moth with one wing. He once caught a mouse and cut off its front legs with a pen knife. Injured it just enough to keep it from dying yet still moving. He would charge the other kids 50 cents to see his shows, witness his cruelty, and live vicariously through him. It gave him a perverse thrill to be able to shock the other kids like he did. It wasn't too surprising that Danny acted out this way. You are what you've been made to be and Danny had been sexually abused as a six-year-old child. He was an easy target. As a boy he was pliable and quiet. He never told anyone about Uncle Jack's advances. About what he was made to do and the awful promises he was made to keep. But it was around the tenth time it happened that something snapped inside of him. Something coldly determined and single-minded. On the tenth time it happened he moved swiftly and without warning. Uncle Jack's cock was almost severed clean through. When the bite was over his penis was dangling by a single strip of muscle and sinew. Little razor-sharp baby-tooth teeth marks all the way around the shaft. Just one determined bite is all it took. He was beaten to an inch of his life. But after that, he was left alone.

Flo hadn't always been a stripper. She hadn't always been anything. She was like a chameleon constantly changing her skins. She invented elaborate stories for herself. Why not? Life could be hard and cruel so why not imagine a life you wished you could have instead of the one you did. She once told friends at school she was the granddaughter of a great Indian chief. One of the last remaining Cheyenne tribes. Her French-Canadian roots had imbued her with a somewhat swarthy countenance, so it wasn't too far-fetched - a half-breed, Metis, at least. She said her great grandfather had fought at the Battle of the Little Big Horn, he was the one who killed General Custer. Scalped him. She said she had a lock of Custer's hair to prove it. Sure enough she would produce a long lock of hair she kept inside a carefully folded handkerchief and would show it to anyone who listened to her tale. It still had dried blood caked on it. Her story never failed to thrill. The hair she showed was from her own head dyed using beetroot juice and cola. But people would believe her story none-the-less. And why not, it was impressive, and people always want to believe in something extraordinary.

She lived with her father who suffered from emphysema, the result of delicate lungs exasperated by a lifetime of smoking and drinking. Her mother had disappeared years before. One day she just up and left. No warning. No goodbye. Flo got one letter from her postmarked from Alaska, in it she talked about the cold winters, the isolation, a fisherman called Yves. But that one letter had been years ago. She'd had nothing since. Her father could barely leave the house, his lungs were too weak, so Flo became the breadwinner from a very young age. She did what she could to make ends meet but things were always tight. So she lied to the social assistance people claiming to have two younger Brothers, Keegan and Kenny. She would always accentuate her limp when she went into the social services office downtown; it somehow made her seem more believable. For a while it worked. They upped their monthly welfare cheques. With real Kraft mac and cheese dinners and mandarin oranges for her, and gin and brandy for Pops, they lived high on the hog for a couple of months. Until a social worker came by one day, discovered the truth. There was no Keegan or Kenny, just an old mangy cat called Hoover. Flo was too young to be charged with fraud, she was still a minor at the time. She and her dad moved on after that, set up home in another town. Waukegan, Illinois. It was there she met a trucker named Ray. He had money, owned his own rig and had a tattoo of a black widow spider on his neck. He would bring home Tim Horton donuts when he made treks across the Canadian border and back. He would show up straight from the road, parking his rig on their front lawn, with a bottle of Jack Daniels, the Timmy's and a 6-pack of Bud for Pops; he was always a welcome sight. The hapless Ray soon got Flo pregnant, proposed and the two married. It didn't last though. Flo miscarried and it turned out Ray was a jealous type - he didn't like Flo socialising while he was gone. Liked her in the house awaiting his return. But Flo was no wallflower. She was no victim either - she was too street-wise for that. Ray came home early one time, found her out back of the shed, giving a hand job to a local mill worker. A little pocket money on the side. She got a licking that left her with a broken arm and black eye. Ray's abusive streak ran in his family. But something had to be done. So Flo got a girlfriend to come round one night and the two partied with Ray until he was drunk and stupid, then the two set about to set him up, incriminate him. It was easy. Ray was an idiot. He was charged with rape and put away for eight years. He swore he'd come and get here once he was out. But Flo just looked him squarely in the eye, cold and unwavering, and dared him to fucking try. How to lie and manipulate. Flo was a master and learned this from an early age.

Flo started slinging beer at Abe's shortly after Ray left but soon saw how much more money the girls made for taking off their clothes. It was a no-brainer. But there was her prosthetic to consider, who would pay to see a crippled stripper? She'd have to come up with a different angle if she wanted to be given a shot. She showed Dwayne, the manager, what she could do with ping pong balls and sealed the deal with a blow job in his pick-up truck. He tasted like gasoline and salt. But it wasn't too repulsive. He gave her the job, a week to see what she could do. She cut her hair and dyed it red and christened herself Candy Floss. She started stripping the following night. It didn't bother her to be naked in front of men. She actually relished it. She felt a perverse sense of power and control. All those leering slavering idiots barely able to keep it in their pants. Men just like Ray. Pathetic. She worked it to her advantage, made them beg for every close-up look at her most intimate parts. Nothing was sacred if it could raise a dollar or two. Flo had lost her leg to a childhood accident, they had to amputate in order to save her. It seemed to her that life was always like that. Always something being cut off or taken away. Of course it was difficult at first, but she soon adjusted, made the most of things. She was a survivor, if nothing else. She soon learned to embrace being a physical outcast - she wore it with pride. Besides, she found that being a cripple had its advantages, least of all that people used to underestimate her.

The killings that summer in Waukegan took the whole town by surprise. Three murders in July and four in August. For a city of 80,000 they were hard figures to take in. There was no particular pattern, no particular demographic targeted. Both men and women were amongst the victims. Nothing to connect them to each other, except that every single one of them had their throat slit open from ear to ear. There was no sign of a struggle. No evidence of forced entry. No robbery, no rape, no multiple stab wounds, no bloody messages left scribbled on a bedroom wall. No weirdo cutting off and taking of body parts. These killings were clean, clinical, almost strangely civil. Yet this was clearly the work of one twisted mind. A single methodical serial killer.

Danny hadn't had a dream in many years. Least not one he could remember. As a young boy he used to dream all the time. Vivid dreams of flying and falling. Dreams of swimming under water for hours without needing to breathe. But that came to an end once the abuse started. After the very first night his uncle forced himself upon him with a brutality and sexual perversion no six-year-old could possibly prepare for, his nighttime hallucinations became a phantasmagorical wasteland. Not a single dream since. As he got older and began to distance himself from those younger years, he thought perhaps it was because he was such a light sleeper. Never slept long enough to get into the groove. He always kept one eye open just in case. But it didn't bother him, not dreaming, and not sleeping. You get used to anything given time. He only needed a few hours' sleep a night anyway, so he'd become accustomed to late nights and early risings. He would often use this time to study up on things. Things like human physiology. He became obsessed with how the body worked. It was fascinating, all the different systems working symbiotically: the lymphatic system, circulatory, vascular systems all interdependent. He had a laminated poster of an anatomically correct human body taped up in his bedroom. He liked to go for workouts at the gym, build up his muscles, keep himself lean and strong. He became obsessive with sculpting his body. He never wasted an opportunity in life. If something presented itself, he took it with both hands. He loathed weakness. Saw it all the time in the folks he sold cars to. Most people didn't know Jack from Jack and were practically begging him to tell them what was what. Danny knew he could sell snow to Eskimos if he wanted to and the schmucks that came into Eddie's were easy. When he was done they would practically beg him for the keys to some heap. It was almost like he was doing them a favour.

'I hate to let this one go, she's really special, but you seem like nice people.' And folks usually couldn't write the cheques fast enough. Danny knew that everybody has some kind of weakness, an Achilles heel, something unprotected, vulnerable. Trick was to find it. Use it. Turn it to your own advantage.

The Bible seller poured himself a cup of tea and settled down to read the daily news. He scanned the headlines. The 'Waukegan Executioner', a name the press had coined for the killer that was still at large. He was reportedly apt to strike again soon. A cold-blooded murderer, clinical and precise. The whole community was on red alert. There was fear in the air, it was palpable. Nobody trusted anybody anymore. Doors were locked and everyone kept up a vigil. The summer heat had reached its apex, which seemed to put everything and everybody on edge. The killings were having their effect on his sales, but not necessarily in a bad way. Sure, some folk wouldn't open their door to him anymore - not to a complete unknown stranger, but others wanted the comfort of God at this time of crisis. When calamity hits, people will always run towards the blanket of faith. Sales shot up. Doubled. But the Bible seller knew that these were the weak lambs, asking for God's help only when they needed it. They misunderstood God's ways. But the Bible seller's God was all knowing, all seeing. Salvation wasn't something to be taken lightly. Neither was it something for everyone. God had a finite number of places set aside. For the true believers, those deserving and worthy.

Flo was questioned by the police. The latest victim had a ping pong ball in his hand when he died. It seemed like it could be significant. A lead. The cops had very little else to go on. Of course she'd been working that night, wasn't that an alibi in itself? But what about the time between leaving work and getting home? There were a couple of hours to account for. A couple hours she spent turning tricks, making some easy-peasy do-re-mi. And why not? She'd done the leg work, worked them up into a horny slather. It would be criminal not to take their drunken money. Not exactly information she was keen to share with the cops though.

Danny was getting bored shooting at the same old shit. The crows had all disappeared of late and the ground hogs and squirrels were smart enough to be wary of his presence. Popping empty beer cans was becoming a chore. He was wound up, full of pent-up energy, he needed a diversion. Maybe it was time for something different he thought. When Danny got like this there was only one thing that would scratch that itch. He put away his gun, climbed into his Mustang, started the engine and headed towards town.

The victim had been in Abe's all right. He'd watched Flo dance. She'd taken a shine to him, coaxed him on. A lap dance or maybe two? Who can remember? They all become the same guy in the end. It was definitely one of her balls, DNA doesn't lie. Now the finger of guilt was pointing at her, and Flo began to prepare herself for the worst. She knew how life could be - something else would be taken away. The cops were grasping at straws though and they knew it. They didn't have much else to go on. A ping pong ball, a strip joint, a one-legged stripper. It didn't exactly add up to a murder scene.

There was a knock on the door, soft but persistent. Flo had taken a night off work, a needed break from all the brouhaha. She wasn't accustomed to receiving visitors. She pulled a satin kimono over her tattooed shoulders and made her way to the door.
'Who is it?'
The Bible seller adjusted his weight by shuffling from foot to foot then introduced himself in his usual friendly

manner. He held up a Bible for her to view through the peephole.

Danny knew the building. He'd been there before. He'd sat in his car, many times, silent in the shadows, observing her come and go. He turned the ping pong ball over and over in his hand while he watched and waited. Tonight he had parked on the next street over. It was darker here, more discreet and would attract less attention. He turned off the ignition. He pulled the baseball cap down over his eyes. He couldn't risk being recognised.

The Bible seller sipped his tea and Flo cracked open a beer. There was something about him that seemed familiar but she just couldn't place it. She was relaxed by his old-school charm. He really seemed to believe in what he was selling. Flo wasn't much for religion but listened patiently to his stories. She was curious about what he had to say. God was offering her salvation he said. All she had to do was accept Jesus as her Saviour and eternity could be hers.

Danny climbed the steps to the apartment door. This was the place alright. Same door, same broken doorbell, same door handle. There was a light on in the living room. She was home. Last time she'd given him a deal - fifty bucks for a fuck and a beer, a deal if ever there was.

The police got the call from a neighbour. They had heard a sound, muffled, but distinct, followed by a stoney deathly silence. When they broke down the door it took a minute or two to take in the scene. At first nothing seemed out of place. There were no signs of struggle, nothing immediately out of the ordinary. The Waukegan Executioner was impeccably tidy.

Flo was wondering how to get rid of him. She didn't want a Bible. He seemed like a nice enough guy, she'd listened to his story but she didn't want to be saved. Saved from what anyway? Hell? She'd already been to Hell and back. Her life was full of Hell. The Bible seller could read her mind. He'd seen it all before.

The police began to search the rest of the apartment. It was in the bedroom they found her. Another victim, throat slashed wide open, there was blood everywhere. The inspector got on the blower, called it in. They were gonna need forensics and a body bag for this one.

Danny knocked firmly. The Bible seller followed Flo's movements as she shuffled across the floor towards the front door. He began to calmly pack up his samples and pamphlets into his case. He knew there would be no sale to be found here, and no salvation either. Flo opened the door and Danny nodded a wordless hello and held out his hand. In it was a crisp fifty dollar bill and a ping pong ball. She looked back at the Bible seller who was now getting up to leave.

'Finally', she thought to herself. Danny brushed past the Bible seller as he entered the apartment. The Bible seller tipped his hat and wished them both a pleasant evening and quickly disappeared into the darkness of the night.

The chief investigator knew there had to be something he was missing. Psychopaths always leave a clue, if you could just see through the obvious. On the table was a cup and saucer, some cold tea left unfinished. Nearby, on the bedside table, was a set of keys, a white cane and a book. No ordinary book. It was a Bible. A King James Braille version, but one that looked brand new. The police chief picked it up. It was earmarked. He turned to the page. There was row upon row of tiny indecipherable dots. He traced over them with his finger. They were hard to the touch, but delicate too. He wondered what parable they told, what meaning, if any, could be gleaned from their story.

Once the rain began to fall Noah knew they would come. The unbelievers. The sinful. The faithless ones.
There would be panic and fear. All come asking God for forgiveness.
But Noah's God was all knowing, all seeing. The time for that had passed.
Noah closed the door on the ark. The great waters would soon begin to rise, washing clean all the lands and purging them of all the sinners.

Turner

It had been a hard week. A hard month. A hard three months actually. Dave was still reeling from the pain of being dumped. Angela had screwed him over. He still felt raw, numb. How could she have done such a thing? It wasn't supposed to be like this. They were the perfect pair - Mr and Mrs Right. But here he was, single again.
Getting used to living on his own after being a couple for eighteen months. Sleeping on his own, cleaning up his own mess, cooking for one. Movie nights, watching reruns of box sets all by his lonesome. No more women's tights, bras and panties taking up space on the shower rack. No more random earrings tossed on the end table. No more fresh baked muffins for his lunches, no more Friday night Thai noodle salad extravaganza that Angela used to whip up so effortlessly. No more Sunday morning sex. Oh yeah, the best time of the week when you slowly

awake to the warm perfumed softness of a naked woman sharing the quilt. Your morning erection already leading you forward towards an opportune and available sexual congress. The access to easy sex - one of the benefits of being in a relationship.

Dave had just celebrated his thirtieth. Angela broke up with him when they got home from his birthday party. In retrospect he realised that most people at the party probably already knew. She was so calm about it, detached, had obviously been planning it for a while. He never saw it coming - great fucking birthday. She moved out of the apartment the next day, took most of her things with her. Her work mate, Carl, helped her move out. Was she fucking him? Dave was suspicious and jealous of everyone. It was one of his faults, one of many Angela had so eloquently cited during the break-up talk. His jealous smothering attitude, his immaturity, his lack of drive and ambition. Dave asked her if there was someone else. She said no. He didn't believe her. Another fault - his lack of trust. She said she just needed to be on her own, needed some time to work things out. He'd assumed they would be a couple ongoing, that somehow down the road they would just end up married, even though they had never planned for this, never really discussed it either. It was just one of those things a guy assumes. Everything goes along hunky-dory at first, you start off dating, things quickly move on. The obvious physical attraction followed by the meet and greet with her family, you both blurt out the L word, the girl moves in, you set up house, make an effort to put the lid down, start to get a liking for Prosecco and Thai noodle salad. What's next? Marriage, of course.

After the first few days of being shell-shocked-single he'd gotten a couple of texts, Angela just checking in seeing if he was alright, probably slightly drunk, he knew how she could be. Alright? How was he supposed to be alright? He was a mess. The texting kept up for a while - her way of coping, easing her own guilt. Just when he was starting to feel OK - boom, another message. And there he'd be, reeling with heartache again. Geez, he might be able to get over this if she would just leave him alone long enough.

She said she still wanted to be friends. Friends? Like that was possible. Sure, let's just hang out, no strings attached, maybe catch a movie, order a pizza, drink too much wine, end up having feel-sorry-for-you sex. Her smell, her touch, the taste of her everything. So familiar. So comfortable and easy. Then in the morning, she'd just be gone again. Yeah, that happened a few times. She was always the instigator, and always the one to leave. It was like opening up the wound and pouring salt in. How could she be so heartless?

So Dave bought himself a new car. An Audi R8. Cherry Red. You couldn't call it a midlife thing, he wasn't old enough. No, this was purely a breakup thing, make yourself feel better thing, trying to move on with life thing. He traded in the old beater, the one he got second hand off her brother, and bought this one brand new from a dealership. Financed the whole thing. Big monthly payments but screw it, it was worth it. First time he'd ever owned a new set of wheels. It was like a dream come true. She was shiny and sleek, drove like the wind and handled like a dream. There is something so satisfying about driving off the lot with a pedometer that reads a mere thirty-seven miles. Thirty-seven miles! C'mon, when was the last time you saw less than six digits on a pedometer? And there was that new car smell. Hard to define, but clean and fresh and definitely alluring. Yeah, a cool new set of wheels was just what he needed to help get over Ang.

Dave decided to take a road trip. Take her for a test drive. He hadn't been away for ages, it would do him good. Shake off the cobwebs. Break her in proper and see what she was capable of. Maybe Liverpool or Manchester - that would be a decent enough drive. There was a cool music scene in both, so he'd have plenty to do when he got there to take his mind off things. He threw together an overnight bag, dropped it on the back seat, grabbed a takeaway Java, punched his destination into the Satnav and hit the road. There is something assuredly romantic and nostalgic about a road trip. Something so freeing. It's something about the movement of the vehicle, the miles passing you by, almost like some cinematic dreamscape running by your window. You knew that life would still be there, waiting for you when you got back, but for a while the future was unwritten. Unknown. Just you and the open road.

He was a little taken back when she first spoke.

'In one-hundred yards merge to the right.'

It wasn't what she said, but how she said it. The tone, the sound, the nuance of the voice. This voice didn't sound computerised at all. This voice sounded almost real.

'In twenty-five yards merge to the right.'

It was more singsong the second time. Conversational. Expressive. My, technology sure has come a long way, thought Dave. Gone was the slightly pixilated Steven Hawkins sound of old Satnav technology, this was something completely new. Sexy. Wow, German engineering indeed!

'In twenty-two miles take exit three fifty-seven.'

She sounded so friendly, chilled-out, and very soothing. She had a slight alto drawl to her voice too - a little Kathleen Turner-like. Dave had always had a thing for Kathleen Turner, had done since that 80s film, what was it called? Body Heat – yeah, that was it. She was so hot in that. Well, what a pleasant surprise. This was the first time Dave had needed to use the Satnav. He'd had no idea. Oh, he was gonna enjoy this trip alright, a sexy-voiced Satnav steering him all the way there and back. Who needed a girlfriend?

'Well, let's get this road trip started then shall we Turner?' said Dave, christening her after the husky-voiced actress. He smiled quietly to himself and settled back into the comfort of the new leather upholstery as the picturesque countryside went rushing by.

'In seventeen miles take exit three fifty-seven.'

The smile hardly left Dave's face the entire trip. All the way Turner made suggestions, corrected wrong turns, adjusted the journey for those detours and unexpected road works.

'Make a U-turn and head back to the A34. Take the second exit and we'll be back on course.'

Her soothing tones and seductive manner practically entranced Dave. He could almost imagine what she looked like. Finally, after a couple of joyfully carefree hours of driving Dave pulled into the outskirts of Manchester. He turned off at a petrol station to refuel and Google a place to stay. He pulled out his iPhone and dialed in some wi-fi, 'OK, let's see . . . TripAdvisor, let's find a cheap place to stay within walking distance of downtown.'

'Can I make a suggestion Dave? I know a few places that might be perfect.'

What's this?! Super-smart technology? Did the car just initiate a conversation?

'You do huh?'

'Yes. I can help you out Dave, if you want me to?'

'Hey, how did you know my name?'

'How did you know mine?'

'You mean, you really are called Turner?'

'I can be anything you want Dave.'

'Oh, you have a sense of humour do you?'

'Of course.'

'Hey, how come you sound so . . . sexy?'

'You'd rather I didn't? Would you prefer a male voice Dave?'

'No no. I like your voice.'

'I know you do Dave. I'm just teasing you.'

'And you tease as well?'

'I can do a lot of things Dave. Now if you push my button I'll show you what I've got picked out for you. How does that sound?'

Dave was amazed. The places Turner suggested were perfect alright. Inexpensive and in the heart of the city. Dave checked into a funky B&B, changed his shirt and then went out for a curry and few beers. After that he checked out the music scene in a downtown nightclub. The DJ was spinning some cool electro beats and the place was filled with hungry looking females. They all looked like they were on the prowl, dressed to the nines, wearing loads of makeup, skin-tight dresses, and those ridiculous heels.

'I must be getting old', thought Dave to himself, 'I don't fancy a single one.' He tried to relax, settle into the ambience, take in the music, but all night he couldn't stop thinking about just one thing.

Turner.

That voice was stuck inside his head. He finished his drink and left the club, picked up a few beers and headed back towards his lodgings. As he crossed the parking lot he passed his car. There she was. Dark and shapely and sparkling in the moonlight. He stopped. Thought about it for a moment, then unlocked the door and got inside. The leather was cool to the touch. He put the key in the ignition, pressed the start button and soon the car began to gently purr. Dave sat back for a moment and cracked open a beer. He took a long sip and then fired up the Satnav.

'Good evening, Dave. Hope you found everything to your liking?'

'Yeah, everything is great. Thanks.'

'My pleasure. Do you want to go somewhere tonight?'

'No. I just thought I'd . . . well you know, sit here for a bit.'

'Well, I'd say you're in the driving seat Dave.'

'Yeah, I guess I am. You don't mind if we just hang out then?'

'Anything you want, you just have to ask.'

'Anything?'

'Well, I'm not much good at scrambled eggs, but I'm sure that most anything else could be arranged.'

'Oh really, anything huh?'

Dave's phone began to vibrate - a text. He yanked his phone out of his pocket and read the message. It was Angela:

'Hi, I just tried to call, you didn't answer. Are you around? Ang xo'

Turner asked, 'is everything alright Dave?' Dave suddenly felt awkward. A strange mix of guilt and a twinge of embarrassment. At what? His Ex calling while he was sitting in a darkened car alone, drinking a beer, and flirting with his Satnav? OK so maybe this did seem just a little weird.

'Everything is fine. Just a message from an old flame,' said Dave.

'Do you need to call her back?' asked Turner.

'No. Not tonight. Not right now.'

'OK Dave. Do we have plans for tomorrow?'

'Yeah, I thought we'd head out on another road trip, take in the sights – was thinking maybe Liverpool. Get an early start.'

'Sounds like fun. Liverpool is a great town. Will you be staying overnight?'

'Yeah, maybe. We'll see.' Dave drained his beer and decided it was time to get inside.

'Well, I'd better be going, early start tomorrow. So, err, it's goodnight then?'

'Goodnight Dave. Pleasant dreams.'

Dave woke the next day a little groggy and crawled out of bed to do his morning business. As he stood there emptying his bladder into the porcelain bowl his first thought of the day was of Turner. That sexy voice, her presence, her sense of humour. She was stuck inside his head. This was crazy he thought, get a grip Dave, it's a bloody car for Christ sakes. He heard his phone going - another text. Oh no, not Angela again. Jesus Christ! He picked it up and checked.

'Good morning, Dave. Hope you slept well. You wanted to start early today. Ready whenever you are. Turner x.'

'What the . . .?'

But Dave felt a strange excitement in the pit of his stomach, like you do when you've just met that someone special and you can't wait to see them again. Weird or not, Dave thought to himself, 'what the fuck', and he texted back, 'yeah, see you in about twenty.' Just time for a quick shower, pack up his shit, and grab a coffee.

Dave hurried to the car. He slid into the driver's seat and stroked the dashboard with his hand. It was smooth and cool to the touch. He started the ignition, and there she was. Turner. Willing, ready, and oh so able.

'Hi Dave, so off to Liverpool?'

'You know I was kinda thinking we might do something a little different. Something out in the country. Take in some nice scenery, was thinking maybe Wales? You ever been to Wales, Turner?'

'Hmm, sounds lovely. You're quite a romantic at heart aren't you Dave?'

'Well, Angela never thought so, but yeah, I think maybe I am.'

'Is Angela your Ex Dave? Is she the one who called yesterday?'

'Yeah, but we're finished. Funny thing is she's the one who wanted to break things off but she still keeps calling.'

'Maybe she's starting to realise the kind of man you really are?'

'Well, I'm not sure about that,' Dave said laughing at the thought of Angela singing his praises.

'I don't know Dave. Sometimes girls don't know what they've got until it's gone.'

'That sounds like a song?'

'It is. Classic Joan Jett. Would you like to hear it Dave?'

'Tell you what Turner. It looks like it's gonna be a mighty fine day and I don't think we want to waste it. Let's hit the road. You can choose the playlist. Joan Jett and beyond. How does that sound?'

'Dave, your wish is my command.'

Dave eased the car out of the parking lot and onto the road out of town. He leaned back into his seat, gently gripped the steering wheel with both hands and let Turner's soothing words guide him towards a new, as yet undiscovered, destination. Dave merged the car onto the motorway and Turner soon had the playlist dialed – ABC's *The Look of Love* pumping out of the car's speakers. Dave eased the car into overdrive, and with the widest grin on his face, he couldn't help but to sing along at the top of his lungs,

When your world is full of strange arrangements
and gravity won't pull you through
you know you're missing out on something
well that something depends on you

Over the next month or so Dave took the car out on numerous road trips. Turner was always there. Not only guiding the journey, making sure they arrived safely, but listening to Dave's every thought, his dreams, his desires. Turner became his confidante, his sounding board, his companion and friend. Best thing was she always listened without prejudice. She didn't judge, didn't criticize, she just listened. Not like Angela. It was on a trip to the Lake District when things moved on to the next level. They were playing a game of truth or dare.

'So Turner, truth or dare?'
'Truth Dave.'
'What would you look like if you could?'
'That's easy. I'd say I'm a classic all the way. Like Marilyn's younger sister.'
'Turner Monroe huh? I like it.'
'OK Dave, my turn, truth or dare?'
'Truth.'
'When was the last time you masturbated?'
'Last night. And the night before. And the night before that.'
'Better be careful Dave, you might go blind you know.'
'It helps me to sleep. Besides it's been a while since . . . well you know?'
'Hmm, did I mention I'm useless at scrambled eggs?'
'Yeah. So, what does that mean?'
'It means I might not be able to cook you breakfast but there are lots of other things I can do.'
'Truth or dare, Turner.'
'Dare.'
'I dare you to help me get a good night's sleep tonight.'
'I told you Dave. Your wish is my command.'

So, there it was; the line had been crossed. In a small village in the Cumbrian backwoods Dave pulled off down a quiet lane that led to a dead end by the village church. He parked the car by the cemetery wall. It was quiet and dark. There was nobody around for miles. Dave stretched out in the back seat of the car and waited with anticipation for Turner's suggestions. Turner played some seductive jazz quietly on the stereo, then with that husky, velveteen voice she began to talk him through their ersatz lovemaking session. It was what Dave had wanted, waited for all along. Turner described how she would love to stroke and touch him and rub up against him. She told him how he felt to her, as she touched his body, felt his muscles, stroked his chest, every inch of him a man. Then finally, she described in deep, dulcet tones how she imagined she would take him in her mouth with his firm shaft throbbing and glistening in the cool blue dashboard light. How she would slowly bring him off. And all the while Dave masturbated while her words, that voice, her sexual sweet-talk gently urged him onward. Soon, Dave lay sprawled in the back seat, panting, and spent. His own semen impotently sprayed across his naked stomach. His climax still clutched in his right hand.

The relationship between Turner and Dave continued to grow over the oncoming summer months. She was filling a part in his life that had been barren and lost but was now beginning to bloom again. Whenever he could, Dave would go for a drive. They would listen to music together, talk, and share the joy of the open road. Through

Turner he was learning that the journey was the thing, not the destination. He loved spending time with Turner, she knew him better than he knew himself. She was always there for him, and she remembered every important and unimportant detail he shared with her. And then there was that voice. Oh, that seductive, sexy, smoky voice. And what immense release Dave felt when that voice coaxed him on to his nightly, solitary climaxes.

Dave looked hard at himself in the mirror one day. Was what was happening really real? Was he crazy? Was this wrong? One thing was for sure, it may have seemed strange, and definitely a little bizarre, but he didn't think he was certifiable, and it definitely felt real. And whenever he was with Turner everything felt alright. Turner gave Dave confidence to do things he'd never done before. She encouraged him to try different things, expand his horizon. He soon started applying for different jobs; things that Turner suggested would be better suited to his temperament, spark up those creative juices. That
summer he landed a job as a graphic designer, it was just an entry level position, something he had only dabbled in, but it was so much more appealing than the drudgery of his 9-to-5 at the Job Centre. He was taking more risks. Risking failure for the chance at happiness and success. That took balls. Turner dared him to be bigger than he even thought he could be. The messages from Angela stopped too. Time was the great equalizer, the great healer. He did think about her from time to time, wondering how she was getting on. Had she met someone else?

Did she still think about him from time to time? Then one day Dave got a message.

'Thought you should know, Mom passed away last week. I'm shattered Dave. I don't know what to do. Can I see you? Maybe go for a drink? Ang xo'. Dave was flabbergasted, shocked. He'd always had a warm spot for Angela's mom. She'd called him a couple of times after the breakup just to see how he was doing. She was nice, kind-hearted and one of the few people who didn't automatically judge him. Besides, she couldn't have been very old - maybe early sixties or even late fifties? What could it have been, cancer, heart attack? Whatever it was she was too young to die from it. This must be heartbreaking for Ang he thought. He called her back and they arranged to meet at a downtown pub.

'Hey Angela, I'm so sorry, what happened?'

'Oh God Dave, can I just have a hug. I need that more than anything right now.'

Dave wrapped his arms around her, and she instinctively nestled into his embrace. It felt so strangely familiar. Warm and comfortable. The smell of her hair. The contour of her body. The warmth of her breasts against his chest.

'I'm so sorry for you Ang', whispered Dave, 'I truly am.'

Angela began to sob.

'Oh Dave, what am I gonna do?'

'It's OK, it's alright - I'm here, I'm here.'

It's a common, yet little understood fact that grief can bring people together, help them find their better self. Appreciate things from a perspective that only death can elucidate. Your world gets shifted by a degree or two and the things you thought were important just drop away. Angela poured her heart out to Dave and Dave was the shoulder she needed. But more than this, she sensed how he had changed, had matured and become stronger. It had only been several months, was it possible? Did it really matter? What mattered was here was a new improved version of the man she had once given her heart to.

Angela returned with Dave to his apartment that night and the two made love like they never had before. It was like a faucet being turned on again. Simple and immediate. Everything that they had had came flooding back. Everything they desired was right there in front of them, in each other's arms. For Dave it was the overwhelming corporal joy to have that tactile love back in his life again. The touch, the feel, the smell, the taste, the sensation of skin on skin. A real woman. Someone he could hold. He'd missed that. And how Angela needed him now. And how she gave herself to him. The only problem Dave could see was what to do about Turner.

Angela moved back into Dave's life almost immediately. They were starting off again on a new page. There was definitely that comfortable-with-each-other thing going on, that knowingness, a definite familiarity, but there was more than that now. Something better and deeper. It was more about the journey now than the destination.

Not only had Dave changed, but Angela had too. Her mother's death had resonated deeply with her. Softened her. Dave stopped using the Satnav full stop. There was no point in engaging Turner in that difficult conversation. Explaining why he had to move on from his affair with his . . . car. Sure, she might understand, be reasonable but what the fuck? It was a car for Christ sakes! He could do what he wanted. He was in the driver's seat - she'd told him that. No, from that day forward, Dave never heard Turner's voice again. It was over. A clean cut.

Angela and Dave shared everything now. Life. The apartment. The happenings in his new career. Excitement for the future. The car. Angela got her own set of keys, and she was thrilled with the new ride, much more exciting than the old beater. It was comfortable and easy to drive, and somehow symbolic of their new journey together, the future yet untold.

It was on a rainy October night that Angela received a text from Dave asking her if she could pick him up after work. But he wasn't at his usual place. He must be at a meeting somewhere. The place was unfamiliar, but he left an address and Satnav coordinates. Angela texted back.

'Sure, what time?'
'5:30ish. Love Dave.'

'Hmm', thought Ang, 'Dave never signs off with 'Love', he always just uses his initial and an X. A little strange?'

At five o'clock Angela bundled up in her rain slicker and set out from home. She punched in the coordinates on the Satnav and eased the car out onto the road.

'In three miles take exit twenty-four', the voice of Turner announced, beginning to guide Angela's journey. Angela was in a happy mood; she'd planned a little surprise dinner for them this evening. Something new she was trying out of a Jamie Oliver cookbook. The wine was chilling in the fridge and the prep work was all done. Thai prawns with lemongrass and sticky rice. She could throw it together when they got home. It would be a special evening. She liked to surprise Dave with unexpected things now. Date nights. New culinary experiences. A special 'I Love You' card tucked into his briefcase or under his pillow for him to stumble upon. Life was good. Their love life was better than ever. Feeling buoyant, Angela dialed in her current favourite tune on her iPhone and plugged it through the car stereo. Soon she was bouncing along to the strains of Pharrell's *Happy*. Not much of a singer, she still couldn't resist joining in with the ridiculously catchy choruses,

Because I'm happy
clap along if you feel
like a room without a roof…

Angela found herself driving through an unfamiliar part of town, roads she'd never been down before. She had no idea where she was, but it was alright, the Satnav had her back.

'In thirty yards, turn right along Andover Road'.

She took the corner and continued onwards following Turner's instructions.

'Continue along Andover Road for another two miles. In two miles you will find your destination on the left.'

Angela glanced at herself in the rear-view mirror, adjusted her hair, checked her makeup. She wanted to look nice tonight.

...because I'm happy...

Maybe it was the sound of the stereo, maybe it was just the ebullience she was feeling with life itself, or the anticipated excitement of the evening ahead, but Angela never heard or saw the oncoming train until it was too late.

Dave got the news a couple of hours later. A young woman had been found dead in his car. The body was being identified using dental records. It would be another two days before the lab confirmed it was Angela. But he knew. The train had been traveling at full speed, she'd had no chance, the timing was tragically impeccable. The car entered the intersection at exactly the same time as the train reached it. There was nothing left. The car was completely destroyed - Dave was completely destroyed, lost for even a comprehensible thought. When he got home he found Angela's dinner ready to be cooked. The wine chilling in the fridge. The note saying 'I love you' under his pillow when he finally laid down, hours later, drunk and in a daze, the bed empty and cold. The next day he tried to make sense of things. Angela was gone. Was it real? Why her? Why now? And what was she doing in that part of town? Where was she going? What would he do now, without her? Everything seemed surreal, desperate, impossible.

Six months went by before Dave began to engage with normal life again. See friends. Go out. Sure, he'd gone back to work after it happened, he'd had to, but he'd operated on one cylinder for a few months. Barely getting by most days. His work cut him some slack. Everyone understood, or said they did, but how could they really? How could anyone? All he could do was put one foot in front of the other, let time do the healing, wait things out and slowly piece his life back together. Eventually another spring started to blossom, as it always does. The air turned sweeter and warmer filled with the smells of honeysuckle and lavender. As the days grew longer and the world came back to life, so Dave slowly began to come back to life, too. He was beginning to heal.
Tragedies happen all the time, to all sorts of folk. People are killed, or lost, or simply fall in and out of love time and again. He'd been there, done that, and had the t-shirt to prove it.

But life was about the journey, not the destination.

Dave decided it was time. He'd already picked out the make and model. Not another Audi. That might be too much for right now. He'd decided on a Toyota - something sensible, reliable, roadworthy. He'd already planned some road trips while the summer weather still remained, and the long evenings beckoned. Shake off the grief-filled cobwebs and move on with his life. He'd never been to Brighton before, but he'd heard it had a great indie music scene. Besides, it was a classic British road trip destination - the iconic beach where the mods and rockers had done battle, immortalised by The Who. He flipped his overnight bag onto the back seat and started up the engine. She purred a little differently than the Audi, more like a hum than a purr. He settled himself into the seat, punched the coordinates into the Satnav and dialed Quadrophenia onto the sound system. What was a road trip without a decent playlist? Then he heard it.

'Hello Dave.'

That voice. That unmistakable sound. Dave's face turned ashen as the blood drained from his cheeks. Every hair stood up on the back of his neck and his own voice became nothing more than a tight whisper caught in his throat.

'Turner?'

Love Locks

Martin struggled with the street map, French had never been his forte and Quai de la Tournelle didn't sound much like a street name to him. Besides, it wasn't a street he was looking for, it was a bridge - Le Pont de l'Archevêché, famous for all its love locks. Lovers, couples, partners of all kinds, betrothing themselves to one another by fastening a padlock to its railings. A commitment for the whole world to see, the key symbolically tossed into the Seine for safe keeping. And in grande Paris herself - *La Ville de l'Amour*. Martin trundled onwards his feet aching from the new walking shoes he had purchased expressly for the trip. The Seine looked tranquil and all along its banks abounded with carefree activity. Tour boats lolled by, joggers jogged, tourists toured, and sightseers gaped and snapped shots of the sights - Notre Dame, Musee d'Orsay, Palais de

Chaillot. Everywhere you looked, lovers strolled the promenade arm-in-arm and youngsters and ageing Parisians alike sat, legs dangled over the edge of the Seine's banks. Picnics of olives, cheeses, rustic breads and French pastries seemed to be everywhere. Bottles of wine open everywhere you looked and people drank from real wine glasses. Red and white chequered tablecloths, plucked from nearby petit salons, created an instantaneous charming outdoor atmosphere. So European. A postcard moment. Everyone looked relaxed, in love. If not with each other then in love with this. The scene. The city. The idea of love itself.

Martin rounded the corner and there before him was the bridge. It seemed like miles he had journeyed from his hotel in Montmartre down twisting Parisian backstreets, bustling boulevards and then along the banks of the Seine to reach his destination. And there she stood, the narrowest road bridge to arch its way across the Seine - Le Pont de l'Archevêché. It was structurally unspectacular and actually quite plain, serviceable at best, enhanced solely by its proximity to the mighty Notre Dame. A few years ago the more impressive and decorative bridge, Le Pont d'Arts, had been the chosen one for love locks, but a structural collapse to one of its intricate parapets had changed things. At the height of the lock mania it was estimated it contained 700,000 individual locks. It was amazing the extra weight and stress this imposed, surely something engineers had not considered, and allowed for, when designing the structure in the first place. But what bridge could have been built with the expectation of holding the weight of all that love?

After the near miss the authorities had been adamant, supprimer les verrous! The locks must be removed. But this didn't stop the fervent love-struck - they simply found another bridge on which to celebrate their bond. Martin felt the heaviness in his jacket pocket. He'd had it engraved: M & J 1972 Forever. He had traveled thousands of miles to reach this moment, to place his lock amongst the others, to publicly display his love for Jean. It may have seemed crazy to anyone else that a man in his sixty-seventh year of life would be here doing such a youthful lover's act. And Jean not with him. Not here. Not really here anymore, in fact.

It was 1972 when a much younger Martin and Jean had backpacked their way through Europe, before backpacking through Europe had become the norm - the gap year as it would soon come to be christened. They had landed in London on an overnight from Toronto, tired but excited to be free from studies, finished university and drinking from the fountain of life. Two glorious months stretched out ahead of them - destined to be the time of their lives. They hadn't begun the trip as lovers but by the time they returned to their native Canada, it would be as an engaged couple. Back home they had simply been platonic housemates sharing a student duplex just off Spadina Avenue, walking distance to the University of

Toronto campus. Martin had just finished his teaching degree, an add-on to his Bachelor of Science, while Jean had graduated with a double major in Art History and Computer Science - a weird mix, but then Jean had never done things in the usual way. An avid reader since childhood, Jean soaked up and read anything and everything that struck her fancy - criminology, astrology, medieval history, theology - any subject was fair game. Ask Jean a question, on anything, and she probably had a book about it.

Jean never set out to be a librarian but sometimes life makes its own plans. Life has a way of derailing things even at the best of times. But being immersed in the musty surroundings of books, literature and knowledge, would fit her to a T. Martin was set to start his first real job right after Labour Day, when the school always started after summer break. He had accepted a position as a physics teacher at Mount Sentinel Secondary school in St. Catherine's, a small suburb of Hamilton, Ontario. Little did they know when they stepped off the plane at Heathrow that Jean would follow him there, find work in the local library and within a year become Mrs. Somerfield. But for the time being, the two months ahead were pure freedom and adventure. And love. They had planned to take in the sights of London, travel up through the Northeast where Martin had distant relatives, hike the highlands of Scotland and then catch a flight from Glasgow to Amsterdam. After that there was only a vague itinerary. Armed with a handbook of hostels and sightseeing tips, their goal was to take in as much of European culture as they could before ending up in Paris by mid-August.

Their romance-free relationship back home was probably attributable to the fact they had been full-on head down in books, studies, and exams. Love was the furthest thing from your mind when you have a thesis to write. But now that they were carefree and out in the expansive world together, love could bloom. They had spent nearly eight months as roommates but sometimes it's hard to notice that the person right in front of you, that is there every day, is the one you are actually in love with. It was during a stay in the medieval city of Siena that they first openly acknowledged their feelings for one another. It was a fairy-tale moment: a Tuscan piazza, a moonlit night, encouraged by some wine and the heady Italian summer breeze, the words, 'I love you' whispered openly for the first time.

Martin stood still and watched the crowds come and go over the historic bridge that arched its way across the river. Out of all the cities they had visited, it was Paris that held a particularly special setting in the love story of Martin and Jean. This is where, at the tail end of their momentous backpacking trip, Martin asked Jean to marry him. It had been the final night of their travels and after a simple meal at a bistro in Paris' Jewish quarter, they had spent the rest of the evening strolling through Le Jardin des Tuileries, laughing and talking about the future, drunk on their feelings for each other. Martin had no ring, being unprepared for this unexpected spontaneous life moment, so instead, by a statue of Eros, the night air scented with roses and honeysuckle, he simply got down on one knee and popped the question. Jean already knew her answer, and in that moment the pair's destiny was sealed with a glorious pledge of youthful optimism. It had been forty-three years ago, but here he was once again, in the city of love, to play out the dénouement of their story.

Jean's dementia had begun innocuously enough. She was only fifty-seven. It wasn't classified as 'early onset' - she wasn't quite young enough for that, but by no means was she considered old either. No one could have anticipated it, no one ever really does. She would forget simple things at first; where she had put her keys, parked the car, not to leave the front door unlocked. Everyday things. Nothing dramatic or foreboding until one day she was admitted into hospital with recurrent migraines. The MRI had shown quite a degeneration of brain tissue – a tell-tale sign that, taken together with Jean's increasing forgetfulness, began to elucidate a diagnosis of Alzheimer's. Their world ground to a halt. Who could prepare for such a thing? There was so much to be considered. Could she still work? How quickly would it progress? Was she safe to drive?

But Jean's condition worsened quicker than expected. Perhaps this is what always happens when one acknowledges, accepts, and allows that something is real - a self-professing prophecy. The next five years flew by, as they always do, eventually she did have to give up driving and also had to leave her beloved library job. It wasn't so much that she couldn't remember how to alphabetically file books away, although this did eventually start to happen, but that she was a danger to health and safety in such a public place. One day she found a pack of matches left by someone on a study table and unwittingly decided to set the entire pack alight. She just stood there watching them burn, entranced by the pretty colours. It left a horrid yellow-brown stain on the antique oak tabletop. Luckily someone was close by and stamped it out with a dog-eared copy of Fahrenheit 451. It seemed like the entire St. Catherine's fire department showed up to help. The gravity and irony of the situation were both lost on Jean. The library had no choice; they had to let her go.

Last autumn after four stress-filled years and much degeneration of her mental condition Martin made the difficult decision to put his wife into a nursing home. The simple fact was he couldn't cope with her anymore. She was becoming a round-the-clock concern. Sometimes she would wander off, leave the house unlocked and get lost for hours on end. More than once the police had to be called to find her. One time she was discovered, barefoot, carelessly walking the banks of the viaduct. She was brought back home, unscathed, but without any awareness of what had happened. Other times she would get up in the middle of the night and start to cook something, leave the stove on and return to bed, a pot simmering away. She was a danger to herself and to others, it was just a matter of time until something truly tragic happened. But still it was the most difficult and heart-wrenching decision Martin ever had to make, putting Jean into the care of others. Waking up with a big hole in the bed - where his wife should have been.

The nursing home was nice enough - Sunny view Care Home. Jean had her own room. She had 24/7 care. She was fed, cleaned, cared for in a matter-of-fact sort of way. There was games night, bingo, cards and all the usual old-age home amenities available, but Jean usually just sat in her room, alone, talking to herself. Her much-loved books sat on a shelf, untouched. Martin would visit her every day, and every day she would seem to forget more. Remember less. More of their life, more of the world around her, until one day she didn't even recognise her husband anymore.

'Have you come to clean the sheets?' she asked Martin matter-of-factly. 'The budgie died you know. It always rains on Sundays.'

As painful as it was Martin continued to visit and would bring things from home: old photographs, Jean's favourite music, small knickknacks, anything to try to prod her mind into a spark of recognition.

'Do you remember this my love?' and he would show her a small piece of embroidery she had done for one of the children's rooms. Something that surely held the essence of their lives together, something she could touch, feel and hold. But nothing provoked a response. She was lost to him.

Martin slowly made his way along the railings of the bridge. There was a multitude of locks fastened to what seemed like every vacant piece of railing. What a glorious sight, thought Martin, just as he had imagined it would be, a spontaneous, heartfelt, monument to love. In that moment he knew this was the right thing to do. He looked around, here he was, back in Paris again. The city had changed though. There were still all the usual Gothic buildings and landmarks and so forth, but something was fundamentally different. Maybe the whole world had changed he thought. Everywhere he looked couples posed for photos making faces and pressing buttons on their ubiquitous phones. People seemed more intent on capturing and posting their love than experiencing it. Phones and hard drives overflowing with never-looked-at-again photos of the world's most famous landmarks. The age of the selfie, quick, convenient and disposable. Did anyone take the time to actually relish life anymore? Somehow this seemed out of step with the old-fashioned romance of a bridge full of love locks. He pulled his out, read the words once more and searched for a place to fasten it. Although she hadn't understood him when he said it, he had shared with Jean every detail of this trip and showed her the inscription on the back. He even brought her some pictures of their first backpacking adventure together; the two of them beaming like Cheshire cats, in love and newly betrothed, the Eiffel Tower lit up behind them. But Jean just looked right through him. Another woman standing in for the one he had lost.

'Bingo tonight. It's going to rain you know.'

Martin spied a small space and began to unfasten the padlock when he felt a strong hand on his shoulder.

'Excusez-moi Monsieur, vous n'êtes pas autorisé à le faire ici.'

Martin turned round. Behind him stood two young Police Nationale officers.

'I'm sorry?'

The policeman repeated himself more emphatically,

'Pas de serrures! Nous ne permettons pas plus présent sur le pont.'

The words flew by a blur, so quick, so foreign sounding, Martin didn't understand a single word.

'I've come a long way . . . all the way from Canada. I need to do this for my wife – ma femme.'

The police officer shook his head, pointed at the locks, mimed them being cut off and gave the universal signal for no. Martin just stared dejectedly at the officers - his plan thwarted at the finish line. He looked out across the river, his mind racing, grasping for thoughts, trying to figure out what to do next. Then he heard a different, gentle voice behind him, speaking words he understood.

'Hi, I hope you don't mind me butting in, but would you like me to take a picture of you with your lock?'

This voice had an accent like his own. He turned around and in front of him stood a middle-aged woman, wearing a large sunhat, loose fitting sundress and sturdy walking sandals.

'No more locks - pas de serrures. That's what they said. I guess it's the rule now.' She smiled and shrugged her shoulders. 'I'd be more than happy to take a picture of you though - if you want?'

Martin glanced around; the two policemen had moved away but were still in the vicinity, so there would be no chance to illegally fasten his lock, even if he wanted to.

'That would be very nice,' said Martin, making a quick decision and he dug into his pocket to find his phone. It wasn't there. He checked his other pockets - nothing. Damn, he thought,

'Sorry I seem to have left my phone . . .'

'Ah don't worry, we can use mine if you like - I can email you the picture.'

Martin stared inquisitively at this kind stranger. A simple act of thoughtfulness.

'Are you from Canada?' asked Martin.

'Yes, originally from Winnipeg, but I live in Montreal now. Hi, I'm Cathy.' She reached out to shake Martin's hand, 'and you?'

'Martin, from St. Catherine's. I thought I recognised the accent. This is really kind of you.'

'Ah, don't mention it, what do you think these things are for anyway, calling people? She laughed and began unclasping her phone cover.

'Ok, why don't you stand over there, I think that will look nice.'

Cathy took a few pictures and showed Martin the results. There he was, lock proudly in hand, Notre Dame and the Seine in the background. Not bad he thought, and maybe the next best thing to leaving his lock here. Martin looked at Cathy, there was a kindness in her eyes, a warmth to her smile. It had been a long time since he'd had a real conversation with a woman.

'You know I was thinking I could sure use a coffee. Would you like to join me? Least I could do is buy you a cup.'

'Actually, that would be really nice. I'm ready for a break, I've been tramping around all morning, you know how tiring it can be doing the tourist thing?' Cathy smiled again and Martin felt the glow of human connection spread over him.

They found a table at the bistro just across the street, outside in the shade. Martin bought two lattes and a couple of pastries to share. It was nice to sit down, rest his weary legs and gather himself. True to her namesake, Cathy was chatty alright, she soon told Martin how this was her first real holiday in years. Since her divorce things had been tight, scrimping and saving had become the norm, paying the rent and putting two girls through school wasn't easy. But she'd always dreamed of a trip to

Paris. It had been a long time coming, slowly squirrelling away whatever she could, but Paris was everything, and more, she'd hoped it would be. Tomorrow she would be flying home though, returning to routine life again.

She had been here for just over ten days and as a self-professed art history buff, had toured the Louvre twice and taken in all the galleries and museums Paris has to offer. Her favourite, though, was the Orsay - the home of the most important impressionist paintings in the world. Here, in the resplendently renovated train station, Le Gare d'Orsay, were the ground-breaking works by the likes of Monet, Renoir and Cezanne. Paintings that emphasised the depiction of light in all its changing qualities. Loose, spontaneous brush strokes that captured the very essence of the Parisian streets, distilling their beauty, the earthy ordinariness, and depicting it all in swirling colours on the canvas.

'I've been to the Orsay every morning. Early, before the crowds. It's been my most favourite part of each day.' Cathy excitedly continued, 'to look at the exquisite detail in Renoir's 'Dance at le Moulin de la Galette' and to see up close the brush strokes in a Manet, a Degas . . . well, it leaves you breathless. Have you been?' asked Cathy.

'No, never.'

'You know I have a few days remaining on my pass - I'm certainly not gonna use it - would you like it?'

'That's very kind of you, are you sure?'

'Absolutely. You can have it. Oh, you're gonna love the Orsay.'

Martin thought back to his first trip to Paris. Upon Jean's insistence they had marvelled at the great works housed in the Louvre. The classics - the Mona Lisa, the Venus de Milo, but they never had time to visit the Orsay. They never got to see the impressionist masterpieces that Cathy described so enthusiastically.

Martin found himself relaxed and for the first time in a long time, just enjoying listening to someone else chatter away. The sing-song sound of a woman's voice. It reminded him of how he would listen to Jean excitedly recall the details of a favourite book she had just finished, 'you should read this one' she would always say, but he rarely ever did.

Martin had been right on time, 8:00pm. He was seated at a corner table for two in a busy bistro in the left bank. Le Petit Boulanger was Cathy's self-professed favourite. A favourite too of such heavy-weight luminaries as Hemingway, Henry Miller, and Ezra Pound. Here the great writers used to eat, drink and discuss writing and art. Cathy had dined here three times herself in the past week, thrilled to be sharing the ambience with such greatness and enjoying the best food Paris had to offer. She enthusiastically offered to share her recommendations for Parisian cuisine with Martin and as it would be her final night in Paris, a celebration dinner was in order. Nearby, waiters hoisted trays of canapés and eagerly opened bottles of wine. The restaurant was a babble of noise as people happily chatted and nibbled apéritifs and petits repas. Martin nursed a glass of Pinot Grigio, the open bottle on the table, and patiently waited in anticipation of Cathy's arrival. He was delighted to have made the acquaintance of such an unexpected fellow traveller. A welcome addition to his plans. Martin sipped his wine and mulled over the day. It had been an emotional time for him. He had travelled such a long way for what some might call a silly whim - a $5 padlock, a $10 engraving job, and a bridge filled with locks, miles away from home. But it was a feeling deeply entrenched in him, this need to find closure, and to do so in a symbolic way. This is where it had all begun for him and Jean, and if he wanted to move on with his life, Martin knew that this is where he could find closure.

There had been a moment, a split-second of recognition a couple of years back, which had startled him. He had been tidying Jean's room when she said quite matter-of-factly,

'How are you coping Martin? How are the kids doing with all this Alzheimer's nonsense?' So shocking was it in its directness and rationality that Martin had to sit down. Take it in properly. He looked at Jean. Was she back? Did she really understand? He took her hands in his and looked into her eyes.

'Darling . . . do you remember?'

But it was like opening the lid on a tightly sealed box to peek inside - a tiny ray of light breaking through into a void of darkness. Then just as quickly, the lid shut tight again. A fleeting moment of hopeless hope.

'I can't stand the curtains. I only like red you know.'

Martin awoke to the sound of a city just beginning to wake up. He had spent the evening at Le Petit Boulanger dining on his own - Cathy didn't show up. There was no text, no message, nothing. Sad and disappointing, but that's just how life is, he'd gotten used to it. He'd finished the bottle of wine himself, sampled some fine food and then slowly trundled back to his hotel alone. This had become the norm these days - alone. The sound of your own voice, no one to talk to. It truly was the one thing he missed the most, sharing his day, his thoughts, or the simple touch of another's hand. He drew back the curtains and looked out over the Montmartre rooftops. It had rained in the night. The streets were wet and slick, and the sun was just breaking through the clouds. For the first time he was aware of the way the light danced and swirled in colours in the scene below. The rooftops - a subtle mixture of blues and greens punctuated by vibrant dashes of colour - the red shutters of a butcher's shop, the towering yellow of the little church steeple peeking through the evaporating mist in the distance, and the streets, slick with rain, shimmering in blacks and golds. He could almost see the brush strokes of the impressionistic painters at work. If he squinted his eyes a little, he could begin to imagine magnificent art everywhere he looked. A masterpiece in the smallest details of the ordinary. Martin's phone began to vibrate. A message and an attachment. The bridge. An explanation for missing dinner . . . a family emergency . . . a daughter back in

Canada . . . so sorry . . . if you ever make it to Montreal . . . . a home phone number . . . take care. Cathy xo.

On the dresser were his lock and the ticket to the Orsay. In his mind he had planned to return to the Pont de l'Archevêché to drop the lock into the river, leave it here in Paris. They couldn't stop him doing that could they? What would be the harm? He glanced out the window, the light had already changed. What was green was now glowing in ochre, the reds deepening into a rich bronze colour. He could clearly see the church steeple now, boldly rising like a phoenix above the mist, majestic against the vivid blue backdrop of the sky. The change of light was so subtle and fleeting. Martin remembered that Jean had given him a coffee-table book on Monet for Christmas one year. It contained all the famous waterlily studies Monet made in the latter part of his life. An artist trying over and over again to portray the scene, capture that elusive light, make the perfect rendering. Martin put the lock back into the drawer for safekeeping. The Orsay would be opening soon. It would be good to be there before the crowds, to have some quiet time with the brush work of the masters.

Hope

Hope. I live on the stuff. Not the real big, cinematic, Hollywood-feel-good-ending stuff. More like the dead-fart faint-sniff-of-it once it has already left the building type of hope. Just a mere vaporous hint is enough to keep me going. The remnants of hope.

In no way can I be described by that maxim, is the glass half full or half empty. Simply does not apply. Nope. I'm more of an if you squint your eyes and stare off into the distance for long enough, then maybe, just maybe, you can vaguely start to see the wavering mirage of an oasis, and if you walk through scorching hot sand with bare blistered feet for hours and hours to finally reach said oasis, you find that they just gave away the last glass of water to some other schmuck who got there ahead of you type-of-guy. Never mind being half full or half empty, just a drop of water will do. From a cracked glass.

Hope. It's what keeps me going.

Today is not a particularly good day. I overslept by an hour. Put it down to lethargy, laziness, a hangover. Pick one. Or two. I was due to open the store a good thirty minutes ago, Ken will already be there moaning on about how this is the third time this month he's had to cover my slacker ass. Guilty as charged. As I stand dripping wet in front of the bathroom mirror, I can't help but notice how the best days of my life are oh so obviously behind me. The protruding midriff. The fast-receding hairline. No more the handsome Greek God, I once imagined myself to be. But I think to myself that youth is wasted on the young, as somebody famous once said. I look down at the razor in my hand. I hold it up to the light. I imagine it glistening menacingly, soaked in blood, life slowly and romantically, in a Martin Scorsese kinda way, drip, drip, dripping from my arm, soaking into the beige Walmart bathmat. I hold the razor against my wrist. Behold death! Could be the day I think to myself.

'Any day is a good day to die', I say out loud. Think I heard that in a movie once – or was it a Robbie Robertson song? Whatever. As tempting as it is to make this the day, I show the world how wrong it's been not to herald me as the greatest American writer since Hemingway, I can't help thinking that the timing might be a little flawed. I did recently receive an automatic email response - 'sorry, but Jane will be out of the office until Monday the 13th' from my story submission to Harper Lee Publishers, so not a dead-end just yet. Still a chance they'll publish my story and overnight I'll become the toast of the literary world. News of my talents will spread over the internet like a virus. In a couple of months, I'll be on the bestseller lists everywhere. Book signings. Promo tours. Record-breaking, unheard of before, kindle download sales. Chatting on talk shows with Oprah, Jonathan Ross. Agents will be sucking up to me; I'll be fending off big-time movie producers falling over themselves to buy the screen rights to my book. I will own a chic apartment in Manhattan and a summer 'writing' villa in Tuscany. I will have a super-hot model girlfriend - no, make that two. I'll sip expensive French wines at trendy uptown bistros outrageously over-tipping waiters as they fight for the right to bring me my food and bask in the glow of my mere beingness. Later I will drink cheap draft beer with my college buddies just to prove that fame hasn't really changed me, watching sports and porn on my awesomely big screen TV.

Fame and fortune. As soon as Jane gets her publisher-ass back into the office, that is. Well, it's not a rejection, is it? Yes, offing myself will definitely have to wait for another day.

See, there it is again – that little bastard hope.

I get to the Crazy Joe's Music Emporium around 12:35 – a good hour and a half after I was scheduled to. Once you're late there is no point in rushing is there? I picked up a couple of Blendz' finest Americanos on the way to make it up to Ken. I open the back door and saunter over to the front counter. I see Ken serving some ageing rock dude with long eighties mullet hair, resplendent in leather biker jacket, a couple of classic Alice Cooper records on the counter. Scooping up a piece of vinyl from the 'as is' box behind the counter I amble up and push forward a copy of Poison's first record, *Look What the Cat Dragged In*.

'This one's on the house', I say, 'anyone with your taste deserves to own some Poison, too,' I offer, sarcasm, just bubbling under the surface.

'Awesome, dude', the rock dude replies sincerely thankful.

'Classic Poison' I state matter-of-factly, 'clearly influenced by the master himself' I note, pointing towards the *School's Out* record in the rock dude's hands.

'Awesome' the rock dude says again, giving the signal for an oncoming high-five.

'Rock on bro'!

I receive a fervent high-five, Ken serves up his change and the rock dude leaves, ecstatically happy. I stare sympathetically after him thinking to myself, ignorance is bliss, and sigh. Ken turns to me with that dull-looking what-the-fuck stare of his, somewhere between contempt and resentment.

'Kenneth', I say enigmatically, 'today is a good day to die. Americano?'

I have been the manager of Crazy Joe's for twelve years now – my how time flies. What started out as a simple post-college fill-in job until my writing career took off has now, unfortunately, become a real career of sorts. Never thought of myself as manager material, but hey, this is a funky record store after all with a staff of three: me, Ken and Gareth, who only works part time on weekends. No biggie. We sell used music, DVDs, comics, computer games, rock n' roll paraphernalia of all sorts. Used vinyl is our specialty though. At current count we have over 350,000 pieces in stock.

Ah, that gorgeous twelve-inch black platter of analogue. A product of pure joy that pre-dates the cold numerical precision of digital sound bites. The loving bump and grind as needle kisses vinyl. The days of full-size artwork by cutting-edge visual artists such as Hypnosis reproduced in glorious Technicolor double gate-fold sleeves. Lyrics you could actually read. The LP experience. Two distinct sides of music to listen to. Side A and then flip it over for the entirely different Side B experience. The days before downloads ruined the music industry. A time when pasty-faced English kids were discovered by astute managers, put into matching suits and given Rickenbacker guitars with which to fashion a new generation-defining sound. Or when peace-loving, dope-smoking hippies crooned angelic four-part harmonies banged out on sun-drenched twelve string acoustics in San Franciscan coffee houses. All acts that would define an era and would become top of the pops on vinyl. A more creative time when artists were born and nurtured and not created for mass-disposable consumption by reality television shows. American Idol, X-Factor. Urgh! What's that bastard's name who created all this crap? Simon something. Simon Fuller? That's it – Simon Fuckin-Fuller. He's the one to blame. May Simon Fuller rot in Hell. No wait; too easy. Forget the fire and brimstone version of Hell; waaaaay too easy. No, let's hope the underworld is one long continuous karaoke audition for every wanna-be-fifteen-minutes-in-the-spotlight turd who thinks they can sing. Welcome to the 'American Xtra Inferno Idol' series.

Check this out: neon lights flashing, cameras catching every plastic emotion. Pretty devil-girls in tight red jump suits with cute little horns and forked tails seating contestants. Lucifer himself in sunglasses, designer jeans and tight white T-shirt heading up a panel of glossy-film star-type judges. Each contestant more ear-splitting and pathetically hopeful than the last. Telling stories about their ailing grandmother, unemployed struggling single-parent Mom, or spastic twin sister who only twitches to life when they sing.

Spare me.

Now picture this - Simon Fuller strapped to a chair, eyes and ears pinned painfully open - just like that scene in Clockwork Orange when our friend the narrator is subjected to a continuous reel of ultraviolence all to the soundtrack of his cherished Ludwig Van.

Classic Kubrick.

But in Hell it won't be Beethoven, it will be the entire Mariah Carey songbook. One ear-splitting pitchy vocal trill after another. And there will sit Simon, strapped in, front and centre, unable to ignore the endless parade of song after ear-piercing song.

Real horrorshow.

That's right; heaven will be gospel choirs, harps and Gabriel's trumpets – celestial music, played by gorgeous, full-breasted angels in white miniskirts and 60's platform boots. Everyone will hang out on puffy white cloud chairs smoking their stuff and enjoying the chilled vibes. Then on weekends they will roll out the rock 'n roll bandstand for that ultimate cosmic jam session. C'mon, we've all fantasised about this. Just imagine the ultimate rock 'n roll hall of fame show - Hendrix, Joplin, Bonham, with Orbison and Lennon singing harmonies. Maybe Jesus, himself, guesting on saxophone, looking 80s rockstar-like, long shag hair blowing in the cinematic breeze. How cool would that be?

But the soundtrack in Hell . . . ahh the soundtrack in Hell will be one big digital loop of shrieking pitchy, Mariah imitations. Forever and ever and ever. . .

Yes, Simon Fuller will pay for his crimes against humanity. Mark my words.

Hope. Even in Hell.

It has been a policy of Crazy Joe's that only vinyl may be played in the store on Saturdays, being our flagship day and all. Today being a Saturday, and in particular honour of my still lingering hangover, I decide to ease our way into things with some classic Al Green. The Reverend himself. Out comes a pristine platter of Green's greatest hits. I gently place the stylus onto the spinning disc and gingerly turn up the volume. Then ahh, the soothing balm of *Take Me to the River* is soon wafting around the store – *take me to the river, and wash me down*. Those amazing back-up chicks singing sweet gospel harmonies to the Reverend's smooth soul crooning. Pure heaven on earth. Those girls could wash me down any day of the week. Geez, maybe it's time to get laid, I muse to myself. For the next half an hour or so as the music plays, one classic song after another, all is right with the world. Strangely, I find myself not only being congenial to customers but also smiling beatifically to myself as the greatest hits collection comes to its ultimate and satisfactory conclusion. *Let's stay together* indeed.

In my own mind I'm already thinking some Aretha next or maybe some mid-period Stevie would be appros. Unfortunately, it's also an unofficial store policy that Ken and I take turns with choosing discs to spin on Saturdays. I guess Ken is still a little pissed at me for my apparent tardiness as he's decided to opt for Rush's two-disc live opus *All the World's a Stage*, which is definitely a jolt to the nerves after the Reverend just saved my sorry-ass soul. Whoa, what a difference a choice of music can make to your psyche. From the soothing salve of Al Green to the witchy shriek of Geddy Lee. Now I'm not one to flinch from a little hard rocking, I can headbang with the best of 'em, but Geddy Lee's voice is an entity unto itself. I swear it could strip paint at twenty yards. And here it comes, the roaring hometown crowd welcoming back their conquering heavy metal heroes to Massey Hall. The big opening guitar chords of *Bastille Day* . . . and then there he is, Geddy screeching at the top of his range.

I feel my headache starting to return. I think of playing the manager card, usurping Ken's choice, but sheepishly decide to let him have his way. Can't piss Ken off twice in one shift I think to myself – especially if I want him to lock up and close down the store for me tonight. Must suck it up and let the little bastard have his way. I knew it was too good to be true; my good mood couldn't be sustained. The glass just drained to well below half empty again. But needless to say I think I'm gonna need another bevy to get through this. Hey, maybe there's a place in Hell for a band like Rush I think, still musing on my American Idol scenario, my head pounding in unison to Neil Peart's polyrhythmic skin bashing, at least for all those die-hard Mariah Carey fans that will undoubtedly be there. They would fucking hate Rush.

I'm just about to head next door to Blendz coffee emporium for another Americano when a strange looking older gentleman comes up to the counter carrying a well-worn copy of *Frampton Comes Alive*. The man is wearing a simple old-fashioned cloth cap, a puffy North Face vest, and some loose-fitting hemp pants. He has a Himalayan hippy bag strewn across his shoulders, and bizarrely, no shoes on his feet. This strikes me as a little strange as it's February, minus ten or eleven degrees outside, and the snow is well and truly compacted into hard ice on all the sidewalks. No shoes? What's with that? Even street people have 'em. He has a scruffy, unshaven face, red ruddy cheeks, and is wearing sunglasses. But hey, this isn't the first time there's been a weirdo in Crazy Joe's, and it probably won't be the last. He slides the Frampton platter across the counter towards me.

'Find everything you were looking for?' I ask. The strangeling barely nods his head.

'Ahh, Frampton's big one' I say, making record store small talk, 'sold a staggering fourteen million copies.'

'Fifteen million here on earth', says the strangeling cryptically.

'Got all the big hits on it', I continue, *'Baby, I Love Your Way* – such a classic song. The first recorded use of the guitar talk-box effect', I add encyclopaedic-like

'Yes, we thought that one would work well', he says, sounding even weirder.

I casually glance at the dude in front of me as I carefully check each disk for scratches but am careful not to look into his eyes. If there is one thing, I've learnt over the years it's never to look a crazy person in the eyes. Don't engage 'em is my motto.

'Well, this looks like a pristine copy, well-played but well-loved I would think. Do you need a bag?'

The man ignores the question and begins digging his hand into his hippie purse like he's fishing for spare change or something.

'Well, it's your lucky day', I announce, 'as all our double disks are on special this month for the Crazy Joe's satanically serious price of $6.66 – Hell of a deal huh?' I chuckle, pleased with the irony. The man pulls his hand out of his bag and without looking, scoops a handful of money and other assorted crap onto the counter. I start to sort through the change and other sundries. Amongst the money I find a small roach, a guitar pick, a business card that reads '*Astral Interventions*' and a crumpled lotto ticket. I also notice that there is exactly the right change on the counter - $6.66. Strange?

I pick out the change from the other items and push them back towards the strangeling.

'Won't be needed these' I quip.

The man scoops everything up but pushes the lotto ticket back towards me.

'This is for you' says the man. He then puts the record under his arm and without another word, turns towards the door and leaves. I pick up the lotto ticket; it's for tonight's draw. A record 16 million big ones! Then I notice the numbers: 27. 10. 72. Holy crap I think – these are my numbers, the exact ones I always play! I know this because this is the date when my desert island number one album of all time – *The Rise and Fall of Ziggy Stardust and the Spiders from Mars* was released. The 27th of October, 1972. A momentous date in the annals of rock and roll history. And that's why those are the numbers I always play. David-fucking-Bowie. I hate to admit it but for once I'm totally gob smacked. I mean, what the fuck just happened? What was that all about? I stare down at the lotto ticket in my hand – 27. 10. 72. Just then Ken ambles up to the counter,

'What's happening', says Ken, 'what was with the weirdo?' All I can do is to rub my eyes and stare vacantly at the swinging front door. Like some ghost the strangeling is gone and I'm left in a state of total bemusement. Meanwhile Geddy is still screeching in the background

We are the priests of the temples of syrinx...

Last year was not a good year for me. In fact, it's hard for me to recall what might be called a good year. There might have been moments. Months even. Perhaps 'episodes of good' would be a more appropriate way to phrase the way my life has generally gone. But if I were to sum up any year of my thirty-four-year existence, not one of them would be what you might colloquially call a 'good year'. Why is this you may ask yourself? Is it because I have some rare weird-ass degenerative disease that will ultimately do me in before I hit 40?

No.

Or perhaps I was born into some war-ravaged country, to underprivileged circumstances, fighting just to stay alive?

No.

An unwitting victim of thalidomide? Cancer? MS?

No. No. No.

Nothing as justified as any of that. I can only pitifully admit that it's because my crappy ordinary life hasn't turned out the way I imagined it would. I don't have a great career. I'm not a doctor, lawyer, astronaut, or rock star. I'm not currently in a long-standing relationship. Sure, I've had several girlfriends, but the relationships have all ended in disaster, typically brought on by my own lacklustre observance of relationship rules. You know, remembering birthdays, anniversaries, buying flowers and cards on occasion. Taking the time to engage in meaningful conversations about work, family, or the future. What else? I don't own a car. Can't afford it. I barely make rent on my apartment. I wouldn't call myself an alcoholic exactly but it's fair to say a good portion of the money I do make invariably goes towards booze. And coffee. Booze and coffee – chi-ching.

My parents have sort of written me off as a slacker won't-amount-to-much son. They're probably right. I manage a used record store for Christ sakes, where the obsessive-compulsive come to spend hours looking for that one piece of vinyl that will make their day. Have you ever spent a week, or how about even just an entire day around the kind of people who go out of their way to search out a classic computer game, or the original x-boy machine? Or someone who comes in week after week, hoping to find the mono version of the German pressing of *Beatles for Sale*? Do you know how many times I have had to discuss with some techno-creep which is the more 'classic' of all the classic Kraftwerk albums? *Autobahn*? *Trans-Europe Express*?

I mean don't get me wrong – I love music. I love talking about music. I love reading about it. And I most certainly love vinyl. But there is a limit to these things and being around these schmucks day in day out tends to take the sheen off a little.

But what about my career as a writer you ask? Ah yes, the real career . . . the successes I have had in the literary world have been meagre and fleeting at best. A couple of unpaid articles published in small boutique magazines (an article about the resurgence of vinyl and the demise of the mom-and-pop record store), some editorial pieces in the college newspaper (the emergence of the nerd culture and the impact this has had on video gaming), one half-finished novel I wrote in college and a few short stories I still chip away at. Big deal. No, my malaise is just me. Pure and simple. Well, why bother showing up for life I hear you say? Quit whining, do us all a favour and pull a Kurt Cobain. Well, don't think I haven't had that thought almost every day myself. But that's where our little friend 'hope' comes in. Just when you think it may be time to chuck in the proverbial towel, a little hope sneaks in the back door just to make life bearable. You know, you make it on a blind date with someone's less-than-gorgeous yet still willing, horny cousin. You receive an unexpected tax refund cheque. You find a German pressing of the mono version of *Beatles for Sale* amongst other vinyl gems in a cardboard box some old lady brings in after cleaning out her basement clutter. An entire box of classics bought for ten bucks and resold for four hundred! Chi-ching. Drinks on me tonight!

Just then I hear the little clunk that signals the end of side one of the epic Rush extravaganza and seeing my chance I saunter over to the turntable. One side out of four is reasonable enough I think. It's fair to say an entire side of Neil Peart's drum solo is practically unthinkable. Instead, I pull out a pristine copy of Elvis Costello's second album – *This Year's Model* – and gingerly put it on and crank it up. Brilliant stuff. Literate, caustic, and rocking. A voice 180 degrees away from Geddy's high-pitched wail, but some may say, no less irritating. Completely in-keeping with my current state of mind-

I don't want to kiss you
I don't want to touch

I scan the lotto ticket once again, carefully fold it up and put it in my wallet for safe keeping. I turn to Ken, who looks
unimpressed and say, 'Kenneth, I have a good feeling about today. Another beverage? Double shot Americanos, on me?'

I open my groggy eyes to see sunlight creeping round the edges of the bedroom blinds. Outside I hear the pleasant sounds of daytime already happening: birds chirping, cars easing their way down the street, kids playing in front yards, familiar ordinary everyday life sounds. People up and about doing everyday things. I look at the clock – 12:44. Sunday. My mouth is dry and tastes like sawdust. Before I even make a move to raise my head I can tell I have a blistering hangover. No doubt about it, this is gonna be bad. I turn over to assess the damage.

All four limbs – check.

All the senses working. Well, kinda - but check.

No body parts missing – check.

Yup, everything seems to be present and accounted for. The damage report done, I think that maybe I should try to get some more sleep. I glance over at the other side of the bed and suddenly notice the crumpled outline of another body sharing the quilt. Shit! As my eyes begin to focus I can make out an arm, a leg, a mop of black hair on the opposite pillow. Jesus. My mind races to rewind the previous night. It hurts my head just the strain of doing so. What happened? Where was I? OK Steve, think. Let's see, Ken and I closed up the store and went for a few drinks at the Rose and Thistle Pub – check. A few turned into several few, yeah, well whatever - check. Beers, a few shots, then what? Oh yeah, we took the bus downtown to the Zero Club to check out the band scene. Ken's idea. Some indie band he'd heard of – what were they called? *Acne and the Zits*? Couldn't have be that stupid, could it? Whatever. More drinks.

Ahh, now I remember . . . the two Belgian girls. On holiday. Out for a good time. Pretty. Punky. My mind slowly and achingly starts to piece together the previous night's shenanigans. Names? Oh God – can't remember the names. I can see their faces, see us dancing to the throbbing, sweaty music. The band was rocking it. Names? The dazzling lights. The dance floor heaving. The smell of sweat, beer, and warm perfume. More shots. Tequila. Kisses. Groping. Names? Writing down my phone number for . . . but shit, what's her name? The night bus home. The slow stumble to my place. Laughter. Fumbling for keys. More necking by the door. Shhh, don't wake the neighbours. The final nightcap of beers and tequila from the otherwise scant fridge. And oh yes, now this I do remember, the messy fuck. The obligatory one-night-stand intercourse, the way it's meant to be - drunk and sloppy. But what's her bloody name? Just then I hear a stirring from under the quilt. A loud yawn and then,

'Bonjour Ste-phen'.

Oh no, she talks - and she remembers my name!

'Morning', I return. She stretches and moans seductively.

'How are you feel?

Cute accent I think, and for a dishevelled wake-me-up-before-you-go-go-look, not half bad either. Wow, Ken and I must have done alright for a change.

'Urm well, I think.' Shit, what's her name, what's her name - think, Steve!

Her phone rings. She answers it.

'Ah qui, c'est Chloe'.

Chloe! That's it. Bingo! Chloe and Margritte from Bruges. Ha ha. The Belgian girls! What does Jagger sing in *Some Girls*? - '*Belgian girls are so pretty, I can't stand 'em on the telephone*'. No wait - that was *'English girls are so pretty'*. Who cares. Chloe is pretty cute by any standard and I could listen to her all day chatting away on the phone with that slurry French accent. Note to self - definitely play the vinyl version of *Some Girls* in the store on Monday. Gotta count your blessings anyway they come. Chloe chats away on her mobile all 'qui's' and 'non's' and the occasional 'pardon-moi'. She even has a cute giggle - is it possible to giggle with a French accent? She seems oblivious to the fact that she's naked in front of a relative stranger. Even though we spent the night together, and obviously did the nasty, I still feel quite embarrassed to be naked and fully revealed in the bald light of day - in front of a girl whose name I can barely remember. Call it my conservative protestant upbringing. Call it my less-than-stunning 'Greek' physique. She doesn't seem to mind though, and I notice, for the first time, the little hummingbird tattoo just above her left breast.

She seems quite involved in her conversation, so I seize the chance to get up and throw on some clothes. The unforgiving light of day won't do any favours to this 34-year-old bod, so I slip on a pair of crumpled Levis and throw on a T-shirt.

'I'll put some coffee on,' I announce, and I do my best to stagger nonchalantly to the kitchen. Chloe continues babbling away on her phone, more 'qui's' and 'non's', comfortable and oblivious, and did I mention, naked? Rubbing my weary, bloodshot eyes I manage to find the coffee tin, scoop some coffee into the filter, and fill the percolator up with water. A flick of the switch and immediately the coffee pot starts its drip, drip, drip. I can feel my temples throb in rhythmic sympathy as the blood starts to pump its way through my hungover body. I slump down at the kitchen table as the sweet aroma of Chile's finest fair trade dark blend starts to invigorate the room. The blur of the previous night slowly starts to sharpen into focus, and I soon find myself quietly smiling at the thought of what a lucky bugger I was. Hangovers can be good for the soul. A reminder that you took it too far, played too hard, are just stupid enough to know better, and after all, it can only feel better as the day goes on. There is something to be said for knowing this is the worst you'll feel all day. I flick on the iPod player, and soon the soothing sounds of Everything But the Girl's first album are wafting through the kitchen. I could definitely get used to waking up to this every day. Chloe emerges wearing an over-sized Pink Floyd T-shirt - which I hardly recognise as my own, probably because of the way it hangs seductively off her smooth round shoulder, her breasts playfully rubbing against the *Wish You Were Here* logo. I wish indeed.

'Coffee', I ask?

Flipping her long dark hair over her shoulder and without a word she silently slinks her way, cat-like, across the linoleum flooring making a beeline for me. I can tell she ain't interested in the dark roast, my God, could it be true? Is she actually coming over for a morning repeat performance? And me, all hung-down brung-down, smelling of beer, sweat and God-knows what else? She straddles my lap and nestled my head between her breasts. OMG, I feel like I've died and gone to heaven - this gorgeous, semi-dressed sexy Belgian woman is actually seducing me! Wanting, nah, propositioning to have sex with me - again! My playlist for Monday morning just got longer: definitely start with *Some Girls*, then move onto Bon Jovi's *Slippery When Wet*, then probably nothing but Prince tracks for the rest of the day.

Hope. Ya gotta love it sometimes.

The television is playing quietly in the corner of the Rose and Thistle pub, a constant flicker of infomercials, news updates and otherwise benign programming. Yes, it's the evening of the same day. The day I crowned hope as my saviour. The glass completely filled to the brim. In fact, spilling over. Perhaps the luckiest day of my sorry-ass life so far. The day I got laid twice by a cute foreign chick. Without even trying. Amazing. I'm nursing my third pint of Guinness - I know what you are thinking, but you can put it down to one of three totally reasonable things considering the circumstances:

1. Hair of the dog.
2. Celebration drinks.
3. Mere stupidity.

Chloe left mid-afternoon. After the sex we went out for a leisurely couple's brunch, feasting on eggs benny, lattes, and croissants. Amazing how a good meal can heal a hangover. Our episode done. Congenial consenting adult sex. Breaking bread together. Then a friendly farewell. Kisses, both cheeks, European style. No strings, no guilt, no problem. Isn't this how life should always be?

Just then Ken arrives.

'Howdy Kenneth, how the Hell are you?' I intone cheerfully.

'Well, is it really true?' He flatly asks.

'Let me buy you a pint my good man?'

'You bastard. You mean you really did?'

'Goodness Ken, it's not that inconceivable, is it?

I shuffle to the bar and order two more pints. The bartender pours the creamy Irish stuff with precision. Not a sacred drop spilt, and with that perfect foamy Guinness head. I return to the table and pass a pint to Ken.

'Ahh Ken, sometimes you just gotta have a little faith is all. Cheers.'

Just as we clink glasses my attention is taken over by what's playing behind Ken's head on the TV. Some fresh faced smiling female host is announcing the results of this week's lotto numbers. Hang on - don't I have a ticket for this draw? I focus in on the TV set then find myself holding my breath. Whoa . . . am I really seeing what I think I am? 27. 10. . . and the final number to drop is . . . 72!

'What the . . .'

'Ken - check me on this will you - did she just say 27. 10. 72?' I stammer.

Ken turns to look at the television but before he can even say anything, there they are - the numbers splashed across the screen for the entire world to see. The birth date of Ziggy! The 27th of October, 1972. My ticket! This is followed on the screen by the more audacious figure of $16,000,000 flashing in bright lights! Today's big jackpot. Holy miraculous Mother of Christ - I've won the jackpot!

'Ken!' I scream 'I've won. I'm rich! Whooohooo!!!'

The people in the bar turn to look my way but I don't care. I start to jump up and down.

'I'm rich, I'm rich - my god I can't believe it - holy shit - can you believe it Ken, I've got the winning ticket!'

Ken looks at me with that sort of stunned look of his. But I'm too excited to care. I can't believe how my luck has changed, how my life has turned out. Is turning out! One day you can be just getting by, floundering in a mere shit-of-a-life-existence. The next day, bam, like a lightning bolt, things change. Luck has rained down. Heaven has shone its light on me. The strangeling, of course! Man, I knew that was weird, but I never would have guessed this. Who could have known? Then there are the gorgeous Belgians. I mean, that sort of shit doesn't happen to a guy like me. But surely luck has picked the wrong guy? Have I changed? Was I giving off some sort of scent? Was Chloe really just attracted to some weird-ass luck pheromone? Who knows - who really cares! I got laid for Christ-sakes, and I'm a rich man! Whoa, that thought suddenly really starts to sink in. Wow, I think, how my life is gonna change now. Things will never be the same again. I'll probably have to give Ken the store. No wait, maybe I'll just work one day a week - keep my hand in. I'd probably miss all those music geeks. Ah, who cares? I'll figure out the rest of my life tomorrow - I'm RICH for fucksakes!

Then Ken, ever the diplomat, intones,

'So you got the ticket Steve?'

'Of course I've got it numbnuts; it's in my wallet where I put it. Geez.'

The ticket, I think - hmmm. Just to make absolute sure, to prove to Ken and maybe to kiss the lucky charm I dig out my wallet and pull out the . . . whoa, wait a minute, where is it? Oh god, I think - no way. Can't be. It's not there. I look again, can't find it. This can't be? I look in every nook and cranny of the wallet, I practically rip the thing apart looking - but nothing. No ticket! I check my pockets - nothing. Shit, this can't be happening. The blood starts draining from my cheeks and I can feel a sick wave of nausea turning over in my stomach.

'Ken, you saw me - back at the store, I put it in my wallet, didn't I?'

Ken gives me a baleful look and without saying a thing I can hear him thinking

'You're a loser Steve. Capital 'L'.'

Then I'm hit by it. A memory. A bloody awful truthful shit-arse memory. Fuck no - can't be!

'Ahhhh Ken, I couldn't have. I didn't - did I!?' But the truth sits there in my mind rigid and unmoving, like a boulder in the garden of Gethsemane. No denying it. I can see it as plain as day.

'I can't believe this!' I quiver.

'What?' says Ken.

'Ken, how goddamn stupid, how abso-fucking-lutely imbecilic am I? I remember what I did. Arghhh, I wrote my goddamn phone number on the back of the goddamn ticket and gave it to Chloe! 'Call me', I told her. 'Goddamn it!' I cry. 'Now she's gone, back to Belgium or wherever, she probably doesn't even realise what this means.' I sob.

'Well, you must have gotten her number Steve?' Ken asks matter-of-factly.

'I don't even know her last name for Christ sakes. Ahhh, how could I have done something soooo stupid!?'

Ken gives me his knowing look,

'I guess today is a good day to die after all,' he says sarcastically.

'Hey, maybe she'll call me again just for fun eh, she might, mightn't she? I mean, we were pretty hot. She obviously enjoyed it too. Why wouldn't she call? She'll call, right? All can't be lost, surely?'

But even as my mind scrambles to cling to the edge of this new crumbling reality, desperately trying to figure some way out of this mess - I know the truth. I always have. It will always be the same.

The glass is empty. I took the last swig. And smashed the glass.

Resigning myself to what surely is and what inevitably will be, I pick up my pint, look at that dark seductive liquid and drain the glass of its contents. Maybe somehow, if the stars align, the ice caps melt, and all the mountains crumble one by one into the sea, Chloe will realise the meaning, the significance of Ziggy's finest hour, and call me. All I'm left with is this hope.

A mere morsel. A vapour of hope really.

I dig into my coat pocket and sure enough, there is just enough change for one more round. I stagger over to the bar, lay my coinage out onto the counter, try to flag over the bartender as the strains of the opening track from Bowie's groundbreaking career-defining album rings mockingly in my mind . . .

Pushing through the market square
so many mothers' sighing
news had just come over
we had five years left to cry in.

Waiting for God

Well, gotta title this 'goodbye cruel world' - only one chance to do that after all. I know, you always said I had a fucked-up sense of humour. So true. But this isn't meant to be funny.

So, a massive SORRY then for all the absolute shit this is gonna cause you now. I'm a coward. I'm an asshole. What can I say but . . . sorry.

Wishes though. No wake, funeral, celebration of my life in anyway shape or form. Fuck that. Don't spend a penny if you can help it. I don't deserve anything.

I did love you though. You know that. And I was faithful to the end. Just so you know. Please tell the kids - tell them I loved them too.

I hope you can find some way to get through the rest of life without me. I know it's going to be tough. I can't quite imagine how you'll cope, but you wouldn't want to have to suffer me owning up to all this mediocracy shite, so think of it as a blessing in disguise. Life has been so unfair. I'm done.

One last thing, if there really is a God, and we should happen to meet, he's got a lot to answer for. I'll probably call him a cunt for all of this. Yeah, I can already hear you chastising me for that - you always hated the 'C' word. OK, prick then, how's that? God is a fucking prick! I blame him for all my misery. You married a loser - that was your mistake. God can own the rest. But remember . . . I loved you . . . Sam x

Sam stood on the platform in the usual place at the usual time. Today could have seemed just like any other day. Tired faces queuing politely, Costa cups in hands, umbrellas, briefcases, newspapers neatly tucked under arms. A sea of blue and grey. Businessmen in business suits. The orderly daily commute to the city. The 06:48 to Waterloo had just pulled away easing itself into a slowly gathering motion and inertia. Ten carriages long, many thousand tons of steel, metal and glass, and once up to speed, not much chance of stopping in the case of an emergency. Sam looked at the station clock - 06:49, just two minutes before the next train, a speeding freight, would run straight through the station without stopping. When it worked, the British rail system had a precision and accuracy that couldn't be beat. Signal failures and other unplanned-for incidents could occasionally throw the morning commute into chaos, but for the most part you could set your watch by it.

Sam drew a sharp shallow breath. The air was damp, heavy with early morning drizzle. Fifty years of life had come and gone and now only two minutes remained. No turning back. No decision to be unmade. This had been thought through, poured over, weighed up many times. The outcome was always the same: life was not worth living anymore. Sam took off his backpack and gently laid it down on the platform. Inside were his ID, wallet, and suicide note to his wife. In the distance, the 06:51 was making its rapid approach. The clean-up would be horrendous but identification would be a snap.

Sam opened his eyes half expecting to see some glorious white light. Or a pitch-black abyss. Who really knew for sure what lay in store after death? But things looked quite ordinary. Very ordinary. A pale fluorescent glow bathed the surroundings in dimly lit normalcy. Office-like. Sam looked around - a windowless hallway. The overhead light flickered and twitched like the bare bulb was about to blow. Sam was sat on a chair, hard, wooden, old-fashioned, plain as they come. The rest of the surroundings looked Spartan as well. Panelled wood walls, a row of waiting-room chairs, a couple of lacklustre landscape pictures hung slightly askew on the wall: a seascape, a pastoral scene, an apple orchard. A small end table hosting a disheveled pile of magazines - Good Housekeeping, Reader's Digest, Country Life, sat purposefully at the end of the row. The stale-aired space was book-ended by two doors, one at either end of the hallway. Sam scratched his head. Maybe this was some sort of lucid dream? His mind scrambled to piece together what had happened earlier. The train station, his suicide note . . . his thoughts were interrupted when the handle of the far door turned, and the door banged noisily ajar. Through it stepped a heavy-set woman, perhaps in her mid-forties, but maybe younger; hard to say as her excessive makeup made her hard to peg. Her dyed red hair was pulled up in a dishevelled bun, a pen tucked behind her ear. She wore a simple shapeless dress, an ill-fitting cardigan and Birkenstock sandals. She shuffled down the hallway; a clipboard clutched loosely in her dimpled hands, and took a seat beside Sam.

'Hi, you must be Sam?' she said merrily with a slight American drawl, her breath a mixture of chewing gum and cigarettes. 'I'm Charlotte, but most people call me Charlie.'

'Where am I?'

'Now if you don't mind, Honey, there is just a little paperwork to do. Could you tell me your full name?'

'What?'

'Sam. Samuel Gilles Trebuchet.'

'Is that French? Oh, I do love the French, such a romantic language, and who doesn't love a good crow-ssant,' she sighed. 'Did you ever see that film, now what was it called . . . 'Amélie', that's it, oh that has to be one of my all-time favourite movies. Now who was the actress that played . . . . ?'

'Is this gonna take long?'

'Why, you got somewhere else to be?' Charlie cracked. 'Honey, you got nothing but time on your hands now - trust me,' she laughed wheezily to herself and gave Sam the once over. 'Tell you what, why don't I leave this with you, and you just take your time answering the questions, get yourself accustomed to things, and I'll be back to collect it in a jiffy. Now how does that sound?'

'Get accustomed to what? Where am I?' Charlie stood up, popped a new piece of gum into her mouth and put the clipboard down next to Sam,

'Why, surely you must know? Honey, this is the afterlife - Heaven.'

'Heaven?'

'Well, that's what most people call it. You didn't think you'd survive the 06:51 did you?' She leaned towards Sam and spoke with a concerned voice, 'you ain't gonna be one of those regretters are you?'

Sam turned to face her, his eyebrows arched quizzically while Charlie continued, 'now can I interest you in something to drink, do y'all like Coke?'

Sam looked around again, taking in the Spartan waiting-room surroundings.

'Heaven', he thought to himself. 'Really? Well, seeing as I'm in Heaven why don't you make it a scotch and coke,' he said shifting his weight on the hard chair, 'maybe make it a double, huh?' he cracked.

Charlie put her hands on her hips and smiled widely.

'Now Honey, I gotta tell you I'm not allowed to serve you any alcohol, not until you've seen . . .' she nodded her head in the direction of the far door.

'Who? Who do you gotta see to get a drink around here?' quipped Sam.

Charlie leaned in close, the smell of her cheap perfume and spearmint wafting over him,

'Big G' she whispered. Charlie laughed, adjusted her hair, turned and bounced off merrily down the hall.

As the door closed behind her Sam scratched his head and tried to digest the strangeness of what was happening. He didn't even have a moment to grasp the situation before the far door opened and an elderly man, priest's collar round his neck, black robes hanging down to his sandaled feet, shuffled towards him. He clutched a dog-eared copy of the bible in his gnarled hands.

'Who are you?'

'I'm Father O'Malley, nice to meet you. But you can call me Pat. Patrick O'Malley to be sure.' Sam studied the man. He had a sharp pointed nose, ruddy complexion, and his curly ginger hair was flecked with grey at the temples.

'And what do we be calling you then?'

'Sam. Are you a priest. Are you here to . . . ?'

'Aye, to be sure I am a man of the cloth, but I'm not here for any of that nonsense. Forty-three years I tended the flock in Killarney. Ah bless 'em, they'll be missing me now, don't you know. You ever been to Ireland?' Sam shook his head. 'Ah, lovely place it is. Tell me, did you off yourself as well now son?'

It slowly began to sink in. It must have happened. He did jump. He must be dead then? But this didn't add up to what he'd imagined it would be like. Sam had never really been too sure what he believed in, Heaven or Hell, or just a forever nothingness. But there was one thing for sure; it certainly didn't look like this. A waiting-room? Like seriously? The memory of the morning slowly began to focus in Sam's mind. Standing over the bed for a few minutes longer than usual watching Lynn sleeping. The steady undulations of her breathing. She looked so peaceful and serene. Unknowing. He kissed her gently on the shoulder. The familiarity of her skin. Her smell. The final goodbye. Then the long walk to the station, the damp dreary English weather covering everything in a misty sameness. The backpack, the note, the timing of the leap. Then the violent screeching of wheels and the sharp pungent smell of burning oil as brakes hit steel. A final fleeting olfactory sensation.

'Yeah, I think so. And you?' Sam asked.

'Hanged meself. Now I know what you are probably 'tinkin, not a very Catholic thing to do. And to be fair, you'd be right as rain on that one. But we all got our reasons now don't we son?' Sam noticed a weary sadness in Patrick's eyes. 'Another suicide - is this where we all come,' thought Sam? Patrick continued talking without any prompting.

'Demons. Life's full of them to be sure now. By God I did try, I swear. I wrestled with 'em as long as anyone should have to. But a man must own what he does now, don't you think?' Sam shrugged his shoulders and settled back into his chair, the weight of this man's confession suddenly descending like a lead balloon.

'I always knew as a young'un things weren't as they should be. Blessed Mary save my soul.' Patrick made the sign of the crucifix across his chest and methodically began counting his rosary. He leaned forward and continued.

'You see, it was in Sunday school when I first knew. And the blessed Saviour himself!' Pat shook his head despondently. 'Such beautiful stories . . . such lovely parables. The Bible is a wondrous treasure to behold.' Patrick gently stroked his book instinctively.

'They fired-up my imagination, they did. I would picture myself in them you see. And always the same image would come into my mind. I knew it was wrong even then. T'was the demons. Once they gets inside you it festers and spreads like weeds.'

'What happened?'

'Ahh, they're cunning and clever, they prey on all your weaknesses. But there he was, Jesus himself, stroking my knee with his gentle hand, all comforting like, a young boy just longing to be loved. Those kindred Christian eyes smiling down on me like blessed rain from Heaven. And there I would be, getting aroused. Fantasising dirty sinful thoughts. Playing with my erection, just thinking of the blessed Saviour having his way with me!' Patrick put his face into his hands. Sam stared at Patrick in disbelief at what he was hearing.

'I know what you're probably thinking,' said Patrick looking up, 'and you're right. It was terribly, terribly wrong. But once the demons got inside here, I couldn't stop them no matter what.'

'You mean you . . . ?'

'Aye, I did. I'm ashamed to admit but I took advantage of my position. I've done some terrible things. I tried not to. I joined the church in hopes that would save me from these awful desires. I prayed. I promised. I made my vows to the Lord; 'save me from this terrible burden'. But it did no good. He forsook me. God washed his hands of me he did. All I ever wanted was his love. But he left me to those demons.'

'So you hung yourself?'

'Aye. I know I'm a bad man. Unworthy. T'was the only thing I could do to make it stop. I only hope God will have mercy on my soul.' Patrick began to weep deep sobs of weary grief.

Sam reached out and put a tentative hand on his shoulder, patting gently. Patrick's body quivered with the release of years of heavy pent-up emotion.

'It's alright. I'm sure it's gonna be alright.'

The door opened and Charlie appeared. 'Patrick O'Malley?' she called out cheerfully.

'Aye,' sobbed Patrick, turning to look down the hall.

'It's your time.'

Patrick wiped his face with his sleeve, stood up and faced Sam.

'Thanks for listening. I'm nothing but a sad and pathetic old man; I don't deserve your ear or your sympathy. You look like a decent man, a kind soul. Best of Irish luck to you now,' he said, extending his hand. Patrick squeezed Sam's hand tightly, smiled at him, wiped his eyes once more and walked towards Charlie. Then the two quickly disappeared behind the door.

Sam watched it close and found himself alone with his thoughts. He had no idea of the time. Was there even time in Heaven? He felt sorry for Patrick; although one thing was for sure, whatever it was he had done must have really hurt a lot of innocent people. Molestation? Incomprehensible and sick, thought Sam. Wow, that's really messed up, I wonder what God will think?

Actually, isn't God here right now - right beyond that door? Could this be true? Is God in the house? Will I get to meet him, or her, or whatever God is? Well, maybe I'll get some answers to the meaning of all this, 'life stuff' thought Sam. Just then the door flew abruptly open and a young couple noisily bounded down the hall towards him.

'These seats taken bro?'

'Be my guest.'

The two sidled up next to Sam and slumped down. They smelled of patchouli oil and looked like they could use a good bath.

'You waiting to see God, dude?'

'Dunno, suppose so?'

'Excited?'

'I hadn't really thought about it to be honest.'

'We are. Ocean and I have been stoked for years. It's the ultimate trip. How'd you get here, man? Was it great?'

Sam looked the couple over. They were perhaps twenty-six, twenty-seven. Modern day hippies. Dreadlocks, hemp clothing, beads and crystals. Real back to the earth types.

'I wouldn't say so; I threw myself in front of a train. How great can that be?'

'That's courageous dude. Wow, no way.' Sam shrugged his shoulders. 'What about you?'

'Returning to the Oneness man, we're all just cosmic energy coming home.'

'Energy?'

'Consciousness expanding, man. That's the way the universe works. Death is just a doorway.'

'But what about God?'

'Dude, we are all God. You, me, everything.'

'Everything is God? That sounds . . . a little simplistic. Surely someone, something,' Sam said nodding towards the far door 'has gotta be in charge of making all this happen? Some omnipresent 'energy'?'

'That's why we're excited Dude - returning to the mothership! Find out what trip we'll choose next.'

'You think you get to choose what happens to you?'

'Dude, we choose everything that happens in our lives. There are no accidents. Everything is meant to be.' The hippy gazed lovingly at his dreadlocked girlfriend.

Sam looked the two over, unconvinced, 'so how did you . . . you know?'

'Man, last night we took some peyote, real mind-expanding shit. Spent the night watching the moon rise, the stars, we became one with the universe. Totally blew our minds. We knew it was time. When the sun came up, we made love down by the river. Ocean is . . . so beautiful.'

Ocean blushed slightly and put her hand on her boyfriend's knee.

'Then we smoked a joint, chanted OM and just slipped into the water holding hands. We just flowed with it man, drifting on the river of consciousness, and slowly drowned together.'

'Seriously? Like you meant to?'

'Yeah man. We had time to experience the whole process, cherish the moment, bliss-out. It was amazing, just like we knew it would be.'

Sam stared at the couple. This was a little fucked up he thought. They seemed totally happy. Young. Obviously in love. Life must be good, right? Why would they want to end that?

'What about you?'

'Me? Ah, my life wasn't going so well. Fact is, it sucked. I mean I'd spent most of it fighting for what I thought I wanted only to find out I was a complete failure. A mediocrity. No matter how hard I tried, no matter how hard I worked; it always came back to that one thing, I simply wasn't good enough.'

'Wow man, you don't need to be good to enjoy life. You just need to wake up every day and taste the sweetness.' Sam looked them both up and down. They looked so sincere. So happy. Oh, if only he had had some of those misplaced ideals, that brazen optimism.

'Thing is I'd lost my job. I hated that job anyway, but you know bills to pay and all that. The future looked pretty bleak. We were in debt up to our arse, not even a pot to piss in. I couldn't see any way out of it. I felt like I'd screwed up my entire life. All those hopes and dreams I had when I was young just seemed to get worn down by the endless daily grind, until finally it was just like that little piece of soap you're left with in the shower; no good for anything - so you just chuck it away.'

'Ah working sucks man. I don't recommend it.'

Sam continued, 'but the capper was the diagnosis. Cancer. I've watched it eat people up from the inside. Turn a vibrant person into a husk. A slow, painful, horrible way to die. So no, I wouldn't say there was a lot of 'sweetness' to taste exactly.'

'I'm so sorry to hear about your cancer' said Ocean, speaking up for the first time.

'Oh, I don't have cancer.'

'You don't?' said Ocean, looking confused.

'It's my wife.'

'Your wife? Dude, you left your lady to face cancer alone? That ain't too righteous man. That ain't cool at all.' Sam winced a little at the bare-knuckled thought. He could still picture Lynn sleeping peacefully, the chemotherapy doing battle with her mutating cells.

'Look, I never said what I did was right. I admit it, I was completely selfish. I was a coward; but it was the final straw. I just couldn't take one more disappointment in life. The thought of the future and not having Lynn. I was completely . . .'

Sam's voice drifted off as he gazed down at his feet.

'Dude, cancer is a gift, a lesson we bring to ourselves. It's a chance to grow; it's all a matter of perspective.'

Sam felt a rush of blood return to his head as he turned to face the two hapless hippies. 'Perspective, huh? Well, how's this for perspective, if God is behind that door, he better have a few answers. I mean, come on, don't give me all that peace and love bullshit, what about all the crap that goes down in this world? Wars, famines, cruelty, suffering everywhere you look. What's up with that shit?'

'Dude, it's just consciousness expanding. The Oneness coming to know itself. Everything is part of God.'

'God, huh? No, you listen to me. God is a cunt! And you, you're an idiot. What a load of new-age bollocks. From what I can tell you had the one thing everyone in this crazy fucked-up world is after - happiness! And you pissed it away. Drowned yourselves? Fucking morons, both of you! At least I had a reason.'

'Whoa, dude, be cool. I can see that you're angry but...

'Oh really. You can see huh? Yeah, I'm angry. I'm angry about losing my job. I'm angry about cancer. I'm angry that my stupid life didn't turn out how I thought it should. And yeah . . . I'm fucking angry at God.'

The door suddenly swung open,

'Samuel Gilles Trebuchet?' chimed Charlie, 'you're up.'

'I'm what? I am? Oh good, cause I've got a few things to get off my chest.' Sam started to walk towards Charlie but stopped and turned around.

'You know something, if this is all about growth, about consciousness expanding, then I don't get it. What's the point? How is pain and suffering expanding anything? What doesn't kill us makes us stronger? Bullshit!'

The two hippies stared at Sam in silence, a canyon of ideological and generational differences between them. Sam turned and continued intently towards Charlie,

'I'm ready.'

A brilliant white light is shining down illuminating everything in a glow of perfection. A young woman is lying on a gurney in a room surrounded by nurses, a midwife, medical instruments and equipment. Everyone present has a specific job to do, everyone knows their role. A young father-to-be stands by his partner, gripping her hand and occasionally wiping her perspiring brow. The hushed excitement and anticipation in the room is palpable. A nurse instructs,

'OK now, it's time.' A contraction. Pain. A push. Another contraction, another push, another wave of pain.

'C'mon love, you're doing great, give it all you've got now, we're almost there.' More contractions, stronger still, intense pain and still more pushing. On and on it goes for a couple more hours until one final exhausting effort before a tiny head appears. Dark, jet-black hair matted onto a delicate baby scalp. Beautiful. The body does the work now, instinctive and determined, nature running its course. Minutes later a new soul is born to the world. A tiny baby boy. Relief. Tears of joy. The pain is finished, the grand effort is over, the baby has arrived. After nine long months of gestation and nurture the miracle has happened at last. The nurse swaddles the newborn and hands him to the exhausted young woman. She instinctively cradles him to her breast.

'Congratulations' says the nurse, 'well done you'. The mother and father stare with utter joy and wonderment at their new little bundle.

'He looks like such an old soul' remarks the mother admiring her new child. The little infant blinks open an eye, but just for a moment, as if to make sure this is real, and then lays sleepily against his mother's warm skin.

'Oh my, he's such a beauty,' remarks a nurse, 'do you have a name yet?' questions another.

'We were going to call him Joel,' says the mom, 'but now he's here I'm not sure. What do you think Dan?' The baby's father moves in closer to get a better look at his new-born son,

'I think we should call him Sam,' he says, 'he looks like a Sam to me.'

'I like that,' says the mother.

'Sam.'

She cuddles baby Sam against her. His little hands clenched in tiny little fists.

'Well, Samuel Edward Jones - welcome to your new life,' the mother lovingly whispers stroking his soft baby cheek, 'I promise it'll be a good one.'

Bruce Lee Lethal Roundhouse Kick

The first time I became aware of it, I made a woman orgasm without even touching her. It was on the train coming home from London. She was a young professional around thirty-five, sitting by herself, laptop out, heals exchanged for coming-home trainers. I didn't have to do too much. I just began to sense what her mind was thinking. At first, she flitted from thought to thought: the day at work, the tiresome meetings with those annoying colleagues, getting home early for the weekend and that rewarding glass of chardonnay. But I could also sense she was horny. I could see her randy little thoughts inside my own mind. I played with it for a bit. Seduced her. Caressed her gently with my mind. It was really just like imagining what I could do to her, just visualising it. It was that easy. She began to fidget beside me, rub up against the coarse fabric that is public transportation standard issue. She tried to be discreet. She actually tried to fight it at one point – poor thing, but I pressed on – kissing her bare shoulders, rubbing the small of her back, gently stroking her between her thighs. I entered her easily then. She was so ready for it. Laid her down on soft cushions of imaginary duvet, her hair spread splendidly around satin pillows, breasts heaving with heavy pleasure. She came. Oh, how she came. In a long extended quiver her entire body shivered with sexual ecstasy, white knuckles tightly gripping the armrest that separated us as I emptied my imaginary spunk into her. Every last drop.

It didn't seem that remarkable to me being able to know people's thoughts. I didn't view it as a gift, I didn't feel special. In truth I'm not really sure how it works. Mostly it would be ordinary and almost boring. That's when I would tune out, stop listening in. I could manipulate thoughts as well, make people think other things. It could happen anywhere, like in the shops or a queue, or in a busy place like riding the tube. Sitting next to someone who would be mentally naked. I would tune in, have a poke around to see what there was of interest. Like yesterday there was this real fuddy-duddy, frumpy middle-aged man, comb-over like it never went out of fashion. I was riding the Northern Line and he sat across from me. I could read him like a book. At first, I thought this was gonna be standard issue stuff - Mr. Boring. But then again you never know with these conservative types do you, they can have real perverted little minds. So anyway our Mr. B. starts of relishing his supper. Here we go I think, should I even bother? And it was nothing special either – no five-star Michelin come-dine-with-me gourmet nosh for our Mr. B. Nope, classic English. Eggs, chips and beans. My, how he loved his beans. Heinz means beans. Had to be the real deal. Loved them since he was a picky fat kid. I could see it - baked beans on toast, three days a week, little fatty piling them back. And how did he like his eggs? Soft boiled. Who would have thunk? Soldiers? But of course. And there she was, a memory of his smothering mummy cutting little strips of bread just ready to dip. Indulging her only son.

Our Jeremy – such a good little boy.

Well then, let's get creative shall we Jer? You want soldiers with your eggs? Then soldiers it shall be. I sent him a thought of cutting slices of Hovis into exquisite army shapes. Exact replicas. Commandos, Green Berets, German Paratroopers. Bready-guns in hand, Second World War helmets on their toasty-woasty little heads. That got Jeremy going.

'We've captured one of the Jerries, Sir.'

'Well done corporal. Where is he?'

'We have him tied up ready for interrogation.'

'Has he told us anything?'

'Not yet, Sir.'

'Well if he doesn't break soon – you know what to do?'

'Aye, aye Sir – we dunk him, make him confess. Permission to proceed, Sir?'

'Take it away soldier.'

Away he went, dunking that imaginary little soldier head into the soft-boiled sunny sunshine yolk. Almost drooling at the very thought of it all. Bless him. Another memory thought – after teatimes little Jeremy would usually return to his room to play with his model collection. Pouring over details of exquisite replicas of British fighting machines – World War II fighter planes, Spitfires and the like. Pocket money proudly saved for that next addition to the collection. Airplanes, cars, tanks, and trains. Trains were our Jeremy's favourite, a boyhood obsession that he never out grew. He had one in his backpack right now in fact. A resplendent 1941 replica of a southern electric S59-SW engine and caboose with gold lettering and ornate trim, accurate down to the minutest hand-crafted details. Oh, I could feel his excitement. To unpack it, look at it, touch it, trace the details with his fat sausage fingers. Oh, how he was itching to christen that new engine, take her on her maiden ride. Jeremy had a whole railway system set-up in the back bedroom of the house. Years in the making, a proud collection. His mousy wife of thirty-odd years bringing him a cup of PG tips and a ginger snap,

'Keeps Jeremy out of trouble', she would chirp to herself while his sweaty fingers manipulated tiny levers making trains whizz round and round through little hand-painted pieces of mock British countryside. A village station, a post office, some cows and sheep standing still in the uber-green painted pastures. Family cars, out for a Sunday drive, waiting by wooden railway crossings.

'Your attention please, the next train is not scheduled to stop at this station, please stay behind the yellow lines.' Railway guards, toy arms outstretched, at the ready to check tickets and assist travellers make their connections.

'You'll be needing to change at Reading, Mrs Jones – platform three.'

Well, let's fire it up and see what she can do then shall we Jer? But first, why don't we gather all the little town's people together, over there, that's it – all facing this way. Now don't they all look so decent and happy. Ignorance is bliss. And let's change the track a little – make the end into a jump. Whatdoyasay? Not keen? Don't be such a pathetic man Jer, you gotta live a little. Just keep those meat hooks on the accelerator switch and wait for me to give the signal.

And off she went, full steam ahead. The 10:48 to Fareham.

'My, she is a beauty alright. Look at her hug that track, take those corners. That's it, around the village shops, past the butchers, the bakers, the candlestick maker. Over the bridge and through the fields. Don't forget to whistle and wave at all the little people – whoohoo! And here she comes round that final bend – the 10:48 right on time – to infinity and beyond! Give 'er some stick Jer – Wheeeee!'

The engine reached top speed and then shot right off the end of the tracks, making a glorious arc before crash-landing into all the unsuspecting townsfolk. What a show. Magnificent!

'Call the ambulances Jer I think there might be a few casualties down there.'

Oh dear, the engine seems to have smashed into teeny-weeny pieces, and on her maiden voyage, too. Not to worry, nothing a little model glue can't fix, eh? Oh, I think I hear the naggy-waggy wifey coming up the stairs to see what all the racket was about. Quick, better clean it up, you know how Edith hates a mess.

The tube pulled to a stop. Waterloo. The doors opened and Jeremy, sweating and anxious gathered up his things and swiftly made his exit.

'See ya around sometime Jer.'

And so it would go, a little perverse fun played out in the mind of an unsuspecting innocent. I leaned back in my seat, closed my tired little peepers, tried to relax a little, but whoa – what was that painful sound shooting straight through my brain? An excruciating ear-piercing child scream!

'Ahhhhh, let go – it's mine!'

'No it's not, gimme!'

'I'm telling Mummy!'

'Mummy!'

'What is it Sophie, darling?'

'Harry won't share the gummy bears.'

The mummy looked exasperated,

'Harry, can we share nicely please?'

'Told you so.'

Sophie glared at her brother and then looked impishly up at her oblivious mummy. Sophie grabbed a handful of sweeties and filled her greedy little mouth and smirked at brother Harry. Harry pinched her arm.

'Ouch – Mummy! Harry hit me!'

'Sorry darling, you'll have to speak up, the twins are having a little spat – what were you saying about Cara?'

I carefully opened one eye and then the other to survey the scene and there she was. An impudent smile on her impudent face staring impudently up at me. Her sticky gummy-bear fingers wiping themselves on my trousers. Little Darling Sophie. And I could see her evil little thoughts, too - sticking out a tongue, making a rude face. What a horrid little creature! And here comes brother Harry to join in the fun. My what beady little eyes you have said the big bad wolf to the naughty little boy. And what malevolent little thoughts you have in your nasty little head. Oh dear. What's wrong with children these days? Where's the parenting. Something should be done. But the yummy-mummy took no notice, she just kept blithely twittering away on her phone. I closed my eyes – focused.

The craniums were fused together, two brains separated by a thin layer of bone and a millimetre of cranial fluid. Two foreheads joined into one large brow. The faces at unfortunate, uncomfortable angles to each other twisted into a single grotesque bulbous head. Oh yes, that's good. The rest of their organs intact. Separate. Fully functional. Which child was more dominant? Neither – a constant battle. English Siamese – how quaint. Little Sophie shrieked first and the loudest, an ear-splitting scream that made your teeth vibrate. Harry just stared at his sister, the shared eye blinking in disbelief. They both instinctively tried to pull away, but it was futile. Oh, the shock and horror of it all. The realisation of being conjoined twins. What's wrong boys and girls – don't want to share and play nice? Oh, you'll share alright. Everything! But you'll have to excuse me, we've arrived at Clapham, and I don't want to miss my stop.

As the train's doors closed, I stood on the platform satisfied and quite pleased with myself. Lesson taught. The anguished shrieking slowly began to dissipate as the train snaked its way further into the bowels of the underground taking the child monster with it.

OK. It's not as bad as it sounds. It isn't permanent, just a little emotional scaring, a symbolic kick up the backside. C'mon, wouldn't you do the same thing if you could? I climbed out from the humid depths of the underground and was feeling a tad parched, so I decided to quench my thirst. Camden high-street. Ah, the Blind Beggar public house - that will do nicely. I made my way to the bar and took a seat.

'What you like?' asked a young Spanish barmaid. I surveyed the selection of ales.

'A pint of Cornwall's finest – Doom Bar, please.'

The barmaid poured a perfect pint, and I settled back to enjoy. She looked me over and I could see I was being sized up. She had built-in radar – who she could trust and who would be a creep - a reflex born from years of working in pubs. It's an unfortunate but relevant fact that you always find the lowest common denominators in drinking establishments no matter where you go. The English pub, the American bar, the cocktail clubs of Tokyo. Alcohol brings out the brutal realism in everyone. I could see she was still trying to make her mind up about me. On one hand English men could seem so rigid, so uptight. Or conversely, when plied with shed-loads of booze, coarse and common – the football hooligan version. Nothing at all like the laid-back men in Spain. Ahh Spain, a home thought. She was missing home and her little brother, Miguel. She was wondering how he was getting on without her. Was he taking his medicines, keeping up with his schoolwork? Things had been hard since their father died . . . her father. A sad thought. But I could see she had already steeled herself against it, kept it at arm's-length, a necessary self-preservation. Wonder what her name is . . .

'Angelica.'

Pretty. I could hear Miguel say it as his sister wrestled and tickled him.

'Angelica, stop it!'

'Come on you little monkey!'

'Angel, nooo . . .'

Angel – for short. She was working at the pub while studying for her MBA; a foreign degree that would have more currency at home in Madrid. I could see her working late into the nights, studying, writing papers - she was lonely living here. But this meant a lot for her and her family. Perseverance. Her father had instilled that in her. Ouch – those father thoughts again. Definitely an open wound. OK – so perhaps I needed a little balancing of my own karma, feel like a decent human being once in awhile. Whatever. There was something about her I liked, admired. She was strong, had resilience, plus she poured a decent pint. I sent her a thought – a simple sensation of love. A father's love. That made her happy. She smiled to herself as she wiped and polished the countertop. OK, karma adjusted, that deserves another pint.

I sipped my beer, ordered another, and pondered the nature of thoughts. Where do they come from? And what about being able to control someone else's thoughts – was that just a stronger energy taking control of a weaker - power and control? I was about to find out. Sitting to my right was a young man, early thirties. Hadn't noticed him until now. Sharp blue suit, polished Oxfords. Hair swept back and sculpted with gel. Handsome and confident-looking. Hmm, wonder what his name is? Kinda looks like a Spencer.

'Warrington.'

Weird. I only imagined his name when 'Warrington' appeared in my mind. Wonder what he does?

'Investment consultant, self-employed, 320K a year.'

OK, this is strange – unspoken answers coming as soon as I asked the question. Alright then, how about hobbies?

'Do you really want to know?'

'What – is this a conversation?'

'Dunno, is it?'

I glanced over but Warrington appeared to take no notice. He was staring up at the TV screen, engrossed in the football match, a half-finished pint in front of him. He didn't look at me at all; he just took another sip.

'Cheers mate' he thought.

'Are you talking to me?' I thought back.

'Who else? You know I tried to tell Mourinho to make a substitution before half-time, but he didn't listen. Fool. That just cost him the Premier League.'

On the screen the Arsenal fans were cheering madly – another goal against home team Chelsea. The manager's face said it all.

'You can do this too – hear people, read their minds?'

'Tell you what Sport – let's play a game shall we? See those women over there? The leggy blonde and her Asian friend? What say we attract them over, just using our minds. No words allowed. See who can do it fastest. You on?'

'Well, I . . .'

'Come on Sunshine.'

Warrington looked me over, loosened his tie and popped a handful of nuts into his self-assured cherubic face. It only took seconds before the two women sauntered across towards us, making a beeline for Warrington.

'Hi, I know this probably sounds kinda weird, but weren't you the surgeon who did my breasts?' inquired the blonde.

'Why those are some mightily fine handy work alright, but I'd have to take a closer look to be sure – would you ladies care to join us?'

It was that simple. Oh, this guy was sharp alright. Soon Warrington ordered another round for all. As we clinked glasses he sent me another thought –

'Hey Sport, wanna have a little fun tonight?'

It was 2:00am when we made it back to Warrington's place – a renovated ground floor townhouse, decorated with a designer's eye for detail, everything that 320K a year can buy. Drinks at the pub turned into drinks at a downtown nightclub. Warrington was a charmer alright. A cocky, confident, man-about-town who made the conquest into an art-form. In his flat the women giggled and cooed and hung onto every word as Warrington regaled them with his stories of money and successes. He cut several lines of cocaine onto a glass slab, took a hit and passed it around.

'OK Sport, what say we get this party started?'

I could see Warrington sending thoughts to the women to get up and dance, to which they giddily obliged. With the music cranked up the girls were soon swinging those magnificent backsides in time to the beat. Warrington disappeared for a minute and reappeared with a tripod and video gear. He began dancing and filming at the same time, capturing the footage up close and personal. The women soon began instinctively posing for the camera. He sent more instructions, and they soon obediently began undressing. Kissing, touching and fondling each other. He dimmed the lights and fed the video footage onto the enormous screen TV. He began directing every move with a film maker's eye for detail and a pornographer's gritty sense of realism.

'Now pout for the camera, bitch.'

He pulled out a box of sex toys and instructed the women to experiment. He undressed his own buff physique and was soon offering himself up for oral sex.

'C'mon Sport, come and get your dick sucked – my treat.'

The guy was a maestro and had clearly done this before.

OK, so this wasn't my usual scene, but hey, what can I say? I snorted a line and joined the dancing girls.

The music seemed to get louder and louder and the whole place began to throb with a hypnotic trancelike surrealism. While I was dancing with the blonde, she suddenly blacked out. I managed to catch her before she hit the floor and laid her down on the sofa.

'Hey – are you alright?'

'She's fine – it's just the ketamine. We can have her later' thought Warrington, 'something sweet for dessert.'

'You gave her ketamine?'

'What are you a complete nubile?' mocked Warrington, 'she won't remember anything.'

Unconcerned, Warrington picked up a large black dildo and began taunting the Asian women with it. The blonde lay slab-still, eyes rolled back in her head as the camera continued to capture and project the scene. I started to feel really uneasy. This was beyond my definition of fun – ketamine? I definitely was losing the urge to participate.

'Hey, you know I think I'm gonna hit the road,' I said, pulling on my trousers.

'C'mon, don't be such a fucking pussy, you can fuck the bitch first.'

'Look, you proved your point, but I really gotta go.'

Warrington angrily pushed the girl aside and turned towards me.

'Listen, no-one's going anywhere until I say – *capish*?'

I could feel the blood start to drain from my cheeks. I continued to button up my shirt.

'Not sure I like that tone, mate.'

'Listen you dumb fuck – I've been streaming this for the past hour. What do you think – you just get to walk away now?'

'What?'

'So, get back in the game Sunshine and give a big smile for all the peeps.'

This was beyond serious. I mean, live porn, date rape? Way out of my league. I wanted to leave and NOW, but Warrington wasn't having it. He began assaulting me with his thoughts. I had to fight back, but he was really strong. I could feel him trying to wrestle me into submission, but I felt a sickening surge of anger growing in my gut. I wasn't gonna let this little rich boy fuck me over. But before I could react and do anything his video camera came smashing into the side of my head.

I sat on my bare mattress, just waking up. What day was it? Who knows? Who cares? Days just blurred into one another when you are inside. But it wasn't all bad – prison life. Three square a day, gym privileges, conjugal visits, Sky TV on demand. Sleeping pills to ease the drawn-out insomnia-filled nights, not to mention your government sanctioned five-a-day fruit ration that could easily be turned into prison hooch with a little ingenuity. A little retail gig on the side – easy peasy. And of course, there was coercing the screws for any of life's other necessities. Well, all that took was a little do-re-mi, or in my case, a little suggestive mind manipulation. Prison life - 'Rehabilitation' is the term they coined. Only good thing Thatcher did for this bloody country, if only Mr. and Mrs. Taxpayer knew the truth. Of course there was always the occasional threat of violence, nut-cases to deal with, the pecking order to negotiate, which could be a problem if you were young and white or pretty. But these things were never an issue for me. It's actually amazing how soft the landing had been for someone convicted of statutory rape – two counts. Oh, and manslaughter.

Well, it isn't murder if it wasn't premeditated, is it?

After a standard-issue prison breakfast we were allowed outside for the first of several exercise breaks. A bit of social time to share a smoke, catch up on gossip, and make those discreet deals and exchanges. I could exhort what I needed, when I needed it. The screws were all fairly innocuous – easy to manoeuvre. All you really had to do was keep on their good side, let them feel like they had the upper hand. Power and control. Not much psychological difference between a prison guard and a rapist. I mean, rape – it's never really about the sex, is it? It's really all just about power and control. Just look at a guy like Warrington, his whole life revolved around it. He accumulated success like it was a prize to be won, and he had convinced himself he was in control of everything. But that's where he was dead wrong. True power isn't about the accumulation of things, it comes from an inward strength, resilience.

Power and control.

Yeah, I reckon Warrington could have made an excellent prison guv 'nor, had he survived.

So, what happened? Well, after being hit in the head I must admit I went down hard. What Warrington didn't realise, though, was not to underestimate a Kung Fu master. Lemme explain.

While I was on the floor reeling, a vivid image came to mind. You know that scene in Enter the Dragon, where Bruce Lee battles his nemesis, Han, in the hall of mirrors? It's the ultimate moment where Bruce pulls out his final reserves of strength, determination and willpower. His finest celluloid moment. Bruce Lee was an amazing human lethal weapon. His poster hung proudly above my bed for years. Well, in that moment I became him – Bruce Lee. And, just like in the film I delivered a single fatal blow to Warrington's windpipe. Warrington went down for the count never to hurt another woman again. I got manslaughter and two charges of rape – well, there was video footage wasn't there? I did manage to influence the jury and got a shortened sentence that will be further reduced for good behaviour once I work my magic on the parole board. Then all this will be behind me. I will get out of jail, pick up the pieces and start life anew. I've heard Bristol is a fun town. Or maybe somewhere quiet down the Cornish coast. I'll blend in. Who knows, maybe take up collecting model trains. And when I write my memoirs, I will tell what I've learnt from this life.

That power isn't about success. Control is just an illusion. The prison system still needs reform. And I will say that the secret to my life was all down to a well-visualised Bruce Lee lethal roundhouse kick.

Disappearing Man

This time the nurse forcefully pushed the plastic tubing harder and more aggressively. Stanley's penis smarted from all the to-ing and fro-ing as the catheter hit a blockage further up in his urethra. It had gotten stuck on its way to his bladder and Nurse Norma seemed to be really putting her back into it. Stanley squirmed a little against the sharp stinging sensation but tried to relax and not fight too much against it - something he'd learnt how to do in the morning yoga classes. The hospital held all sorts of activities to help make patients' stays be more beneficial and conducive to treatments: yoga, journaling, dream therapy, walking club, you name it. St. Joseph's Hospital prided itself on the very latest in-patient amenities and care. The young upbeat woman who wore the colourful leotards had taught all of those pale-faced sickly patients who could walk, shuffle, or merely wheel themselves to the patient lounge, all about breath control and how to breathe deeply all the way into your toes. Stanley wasn't too sure about breathing with his feet, but he liked to watch her as she stretched this way and that demonstrating various postures and poses. Not struggling was something Stanley had had to learn the hard way. Putting up a fight usually only meant things going wrong, procedures taking longer, more discomfort and unwanted side effects, something Stanley had experienced throughout the multiples of treatments he'd endured over his three-month stay at St. Joseph's. Today was no different, but Stanley was becoming an old hand at things.

Mustering what was left of his flagging resilience he filled up his toes with breath and was soon trying to send thoughts of relaxation into the tubing as it pushed and snaked its way inside his ravaged body. The past three months had been a marathon through the various care facilities and latest treatments the hospital had to offer. Now he was on the final lap. He had been moved from Surgical to ICU, and now he was stabilised, finally here, to Green Pastures - the hospital palliative ward.

The process towards the inevitable was already under way. The treatment plan had been amended. No more invasive surgery or chemotherapy. No more blood tests, enemas, and probing needles. Green Pastures was all about comfort and relief. Make the final hurrah as liveable and pain-free as possible. There was art therapy to help patients express their anger and grief, and journaling to help them compose their farewells.

Palliative care; put your affairs in order, take stock of your life, as the body instinctively and surely begins to shut down. Stanley had been given two more weeks to live. Two more weeks? The sheer absurdity of calling the last innings. How could they be so sure? Two more weeks. It's funny how time can be though. Years ago, two weeks used to seem like all the time in the world. A date circled in red marker on the family calendar, post it notes on the fridge, a reminder to buy supplies. A fortnight that was anticipated for months before it arrived. The two weeks Stanley would take his family on the annual camping trip down the Oregon coast. From the August long weekend onwards, the kids and a basement full of musty camping gear piled into the back of the trusty Mazda Minivan would hit the open road, out onto the highway of adventure. Ralph, the beloved family spaniel always laid quietly down at the kids' feet, while Ann kept the vacation vibes going with the mixed tapes playing on the cassette deck up front. From the Beatles to The Flaming Lips, everyone's favourite songs were included, but little did they know that these tapes were to become the soundtrack to their lives. The whole family loved the camping escapades and Stanley always scoped out the best camping spots well in advance. He knew where to find dry firewood, where to buy cheap packs of American Budweiser and cans of Dr Pepper and Doritos for the kids. He knew the campsites that were dog-friendly and also had beach access. The tried and trusted. Fond memories from each preceding adventure. Oregon was breathtaking, especially in summertime. The rugged rocky coastline, the forests of giant evergreens and the endless beaches and coves were an explorer's delight. The annual jaunt was a time for chillaxing, stargazing, marshmallow roasting on open-pit fires and beachcombing for shells, rocks and other prized finds that would end up adorning bookshelves, nooks-and-crannies and anywhere else a child's imagination would allow.

The pain jolted back into Stanley with the force of a hammer hitting an anvil. The catheter had hit another snag; it felt like it was scraping the inside of his plumbing practically clean. Stanley gripped his teeth, pushed his gaze off into the whiteness of the hospital walls and tried to picture something approaching pleasurable. All he could envisage in that moment was pitching the tent. Banging in the final peg to secure the old orange tarp, strung up to construct a makeshift covering over the picnic table, an instant outdoor dining room. Tent up. Sleeping bags unpacked. Everything sorted. No TVs, devices or phones to distract. Nothing to do now but unpack the vintage Coleman and make hot chocolate for the kids, a little bourbon in Dad's cup, and take cover under the tarp. Sit back, relax, and meditate on the gentle Oregon rain that drizzled down until eventually everything would be permeated with a West Coast wetness that soaked through to your very bones. But Stanley knew it was only a matter of time before the sun would come out again. It always did. The rain had a beauty all of its own.

Catheter finally in, Norma secured it with some sticky plaster to the side of Stanley's old fella. A trickle of golden urine, spotted with blood, was already making its way down through the tubing - another tell-tale sign that Stanley's cancer had returned with a vengeance. Stanley and Ann had lived a good life together. They had raised two kids, paid off one mortgage, owned three dogs, two cats, a guinea pig called George and a tortoise named Arnold. Life had certainly had its ups and downs, but they had managed to manoeuvre and navigate their way through most of what life could deal up successfully and with aplomb. Last October Ann had suffered two back-to-back strokes that left her infirm. For Ann this meant her life was now confined to a province-funded nursing home. Stanley was simply unable to take care of her himself. This was the first time in forty-two years Stanley and Ann had ever lived apart from one another. Last time he'd seen his wife had been three months ago just before he'd been admitted to hospital to start his final round of chemo. He'd slept in a standard-issue hospital bed ever since. Their son, Brian, had picked him up and driven him to see her on their way to St. Joseph's. It was an awkward moment. Stanley realised right away that this could very well be the last time they would see each other. And there they were. A right couple thought Stanley. Ann, hardly able to squeeze his hand never mind able to say a damn word. Stanley making small talk with the woman he'd known intimately all his life, like he was caught in some clumsy elevator conversation. But what was there really to say? Pathetic thought Stanley, that life had come down to this - idle banter with his wife. And poor Brian, left to watch his parents face this final disastrous stage of their lives, one in a near vegetative state, the other on his way to his final unwinnable round with cancer.

Brian had taken to the role of carer like he took to everything in life, with a dutiful diligence. Although he was busy with a young family of his own, he still made the time to help out: driving his dad to chemotherapy treatments and regularly bringing the kids to see their grandmother. Brian had become the glue that held things together. He had inherited the family camping gear; Stanley had insisted he have it all. Brian's sister, Penny, hadn't grown into much of an outdoorsy type so the gear naturally went to Brian. Penny married right after university and had moved miles away, halfway across the country in fact, to live in Montreal. She came back home to visit bringing her Jewish boyfriend, Seth, to meet the family. Stanley hadn't particularly warmed to the guy, not because he was Jewish, although he did quite frankly wonder what the future Christmas get-togethers would be like with a Jew in the family, but it was more that he didn't seem to have the same sense of humour as them. Or any sense of humour at all, to be honest. Seth just stared blankly at him when he proclaimed,

'That piece of halibut was good enough for Jehovah', in praise of Ann's outstanding thanksgiving dinner.
Stanley knew Monty Python skits word for word and once he had a few drinks in him, loved nothing more than to

quote scenes and imitate all the voices. Of course, Penny got understandably uptight when Stanley said to Seth,

'Come on Big Nose, let's haggle', over the last Yorkshire pudding, but Stanley was oblivious to any insult his good-natured banter may have inadvertently caused. The family had learned to embrace, or at least endure, his familiar humour but what good was a son-in-law if you couldn't share your well-worn jokes over a bourbon or two? Besides, it bothered Stanley that Seth had never even stepped foot inside a tent in his life. No wonder Penny had become so bookish, living in Montreal, the most pretentious and stuck-up of all Canadian cities. And with a Jewish tax accountant that hadn't the foggiest about enjoying the great outdoors. Where was the pleasure in that kind of life? And a province that thought it was better than the rest?

'Let Quebec separate and good riddance to 'em.' said Stanley loudly at the dinner table, too many glasses of wine getting the better of him. 'I don't suppose you've ever been to Oregon or seen the Northern Lights' inquired Stanley of the sheepish accountant. But before Stanley could put his foot any further into his mouth Ann ushered everyone into the living room, served her famous home-made lemon-drizzle cake and brought out the family photo albums to show Seth some pictures of Penny as a toddler. Penny cringed a little at first but inevitably the stories of the annual camping trips were re-lived and as always, this brought everyone together in a camaraderie that only cherished and shared memories could.

'Off down the old stomping grounds again this

summer?' said Stanley to his son. Brian nodded but hadn't the heart to tell his dad he'd already replaced the old camping gear with new stuff from Walmart. But who could blame him? Walmart was the home of cheap deals, everything at least half the price of a proper store and an unavoidable way to stretch an already stretched family budget. What with braces for both the kids, and hockey gear to buy for Dylan, a bargain was a bargain no matter where you found it. Even if it was at the price of supporting an American conglomerate that had no conscience for the environment. Sweatshops in India were where Walmart got their stuff, Stanley was sure of it. He refused to shop there and would always say to anyone who would listen that Walmart would be the downfall of civilisation as we know it. But the bottom line was that camping equipment had come a long way since the eighties, much slicker, lighter and more compact than the cumbersome stuff that Stanley used to make them lug around. And Walmart had it all. At rock bottom prices. What was poor Brian to do?

After making awkward small talk with Ann in the Blue Acres Care Home lounge, in what seemed like a perverse eternity, a nurse had saved the day by dutifully arriving to attend to Ann's bed sores. Privacy needed, Stanley took this as his cue to leave. There was no point in dragging things out. Enough is enough. Putting everyone through the emotional ringer wouldn't make things any better, or easier. Stanley leaned in and kissed Ann on the temple just like he had done a thousand times before and then he and Brian quietly made their exit. Outside, the Vancouver air was brisk and chill and Stanley couldn't help noticing the scalding tears streaming down Brian's face as he helped his father into the station wagon.

'Let's stop off at Mike's Place for a drink before we go whatdoyasay Bri?'

'But Dad, we are already running late. You have an appointment with Dr. Akbar.'

'C'mon Bri, one for your birthday, there'll be plenty of times for appointments, when does a guy get to celebrate his son's big day?'

'It's not until September. That's ages from now.'

Stanley looked straight ahead and avoided stating the obvious.

'Just thought it might be fun. For old time's sake.'

Realizing his insensitivity, Brian immediately felt guilty and seeing as he had already arranged for Carly to pick the kids up after school, he quietly turned the car down Georgia Street.

'Sure Dad, think we have time for a quick one. Mom looked better today don't you think?'

Stanley just nodded and pointed out a parking space straight ahead.

Brian returned to the table with a couple of glasses - a diet coke for himself and a large tumbler of bourbon and 7-up - his father's favourite.

'Aren't you having one?'

'Driving Dad.'

'Sure thing. Well, cheers then Bri.'

Brian clinked glasses and looked around. The bar was sparsely filled with afternoon drinkers - the gainfully unemployed, the lonely, the businessmen brokering deals over a liquid lunch. The air was blue with haze and the place smelled of stale beer.

'See the Habs won again last night' said Stanley, 'they might make it all the way to the cup.'

'Yeah, they're looking pretty good. I promised Dylan I'd take him to a Canucks game this year; he's so into hockey now.'

The two fell silent again and sat uncomfortably in the gloomy atmosphere for a minute or two before Brian began to fill the space with tales about Dylan's hockey practices. How every week was the same; on Mondays, Wednesdays and Fridays he'd get up at 5:30, scrape the snow off the car in the freezing cold and chauffeur Dylan down to the rink and back. But it was well worth it. It was only Dylan's second year of playing junior league, but he'd already made the second line. His coach was impressed and Brian was really proud of his son. Each practice they followed the same routine - a quick pit stop through the Tim Horton's drive thru for a breakfast muffin for Dylan and a large coffee and honey crueler for Brian; a little ritual father and son bonding time. Dylan's self-esteem seemed to have really grown because of it all.

'Self-esteem,' thought Stanley to himself? 'Holy crap, didn't think that was something that had to be grown. What was Brian raising - rare orchids?'

Brian continuing chatting away, perhaps

subconsciously not wanting to leave any space to be filled up by any mention of death or dying or last will and testaments, he just couldn't face that kind of conversation with his father, not today, not right now, so instead he told how little Hayley had developed a passion for collecting things. Something her therapist had recommended he and Carly encourage on account of her newly diagnosed autism. Last year it was Hello Kitty stickers and this year she had amassed a fine collection of horses; all sorts of horse paraphernalia. Stuffed horses, china horses, horse mask with absurd toothy grins. But her very latest thing was Beanie Babies. She already had a huge collection, thirty-four at last count. Brian laughed heartily and said they might need to move into a bigger house if it kept up at this rate, just to be able to fit them all. But what the hell are Beanie Babies thought Stanley? Babies filled up with beans Best not to ask.' Stanley dug into his wallet and pulled out another twenty and handed it to Brian.

'One more for the road. Sure you won't have a real one?' Brian shook his head and took the money from his dad.

'Hey, see if they have any smokes up there will ya - Marlboro?'

'Dad?'

'What - d'ya think it'll kill me or something?'

Brian and Stanley walked slowly back to the car, the afternoon light seeming brighter than usual after the dimness of the bar. Stanley squinted a little to get his bearing and felt the glow of weak sunshine warm his tired face. He sat down on a bus stop bench, opened the pack of cigarettes, lit one and took a long satisfying drag letting the smoke and nicotine permeate deeply into his tired lungs. Screw it; the chemotherapy could wait a little longer. Instantly he was transported back to the misty mornings along the Oregon coast. Stanley would always be the first up, mostly due to his inherently weak bladder. But he would always make the most of the moment to bask in the tranquility and beauty of the surroundings, start the morning fire, and enjoy that first smoke of the day in solitude. The camping trips were some of his fondest family memories. Teaching the kids how to swim, how to light a fire and how to find a good marshmallow stick. He was proud of the values he'd instilled in them. A love of outdoors, nature, fresh air, and the beauty that was to be found in the simple things all around. He looked at his son, all grown up now and busy with his own family. He looked much more like Ann than him. He remembered teaching him the rudiments of hockey on the backyard rink he used to freeze over every year. Learning how to skate and handle the puck. How to check and be checked. Hockey survival skills. Brian had a natural inclination for defence. Cautious and steady, that was Brian alright, and the traits of a good defensive player. Stanley blew out a lungful of smoke into the afternoon air and instantly felt that same ragged and dirty joy that smoking had always provided.

'You know Dad, I don't think that's too good with the chemotherapy.'

'Ah fiddle-sticks. Chemo-schmeemo. A man's gotta enjoy himself.'

Brian shuffled his feet restlessly trying not to seem impatient, while he let his father enjoy the rest of his cigarette. The traffic lights changed and a classic '65 Mustang convertible rounded the corner and slid past, classic tunes belting out from its speakers into the midday air.

'Look at that Bri, now that's a real beaut. Classic Mustang. I always wanted one of those.'

'Why didn't you ever buy one Dad - you and Mom could have afforded it?'

'It's not a family ride Bri. Your Mom would never hear of it, besides, where would we put all the camping gear?'

Stanley watched the car turn the corner and disappear. It would have been fun alright, to have owned a Mustang. He stamped out his butt on the sidewalk and grabbed Brian's arm.

'C'mon kid, time to get this show on the road.'

Stanley laid back into the relative comfort of his hospital bed. Catheter finally in, another invasive and embarrassing procedure survived; he was happy to have distracted himself with his memories.

'Better than breathing with your feet,' muttered Stanley to himself, and he smiled as the thoughts of camping trips gone by dissolved in his mind. 'Geez', thought Stanley suddenly hit by a new idea, 'didn't Brian say he'd be visiting with the kids tonight? Maybe I can get him to sneak me in a mickey of Jack Daniels? A man's gotta enjoy what time he has left.' He reached over to find his cell phone. On the night table staring blankly at him was a rainbow-coloured unicorn Beanie Baby.

'What do you think?' said Stanley to the ludicrous toy, 'a little whiskey for grandpa tonight?' Stanley smiled to himself. Just then the door swung open and a couple of burly hospital porters pushed a bed through the gaping mouth of a doorway. Stanley sat up a little to get a better look.

'Well look here', he thought to himself, 'seems like I'm getting me a roommate.'

After a little manoeuvring the two finally managed to park the bed in the vacant space next to Stanley's and he got his first proper look at the man who he'd be sharing the same air with for the next while.

In the bed lay a little brown body with wispy white hair that stood electric-shock upright. He had one of those goat-like beards, grey and scraggly. His face was full of deep lines and wrinkles. He didn't seem like much of a man. He was very slight, like someone who was slowly evaporating from this life. He had a tube stuck up his nose and another in his arm quietly dripping God-knows-what into his emaciated body.

'Looks like a little lost bird' thought Stanley. The brown man slowly peeled open his eyes and began to take in his new surroundings.

'Not much to look at', wheezed Stanley, 'sure ain't no Taj Mahal'. Abul turned his head slightly and managed a polite nod.

'You speak English Sammy?'

Abul moved his eyebrows up in a delicate motion that could have been interpreted as a 'yes', or as an 'I don't understand' gesture.

'Perfect,' said Stanley sarcastically, 'an ignorant foreigner.'

Then, with a tiny hoarse voice, the brown man managed, 'yes, perfectly. I understand.'

Stanley gave him the once over and continued.

'So what you got then?'

'Got?'

'What's wrong with you?'

The little brown man closed his eyes and sighed, 'bladder cancer. They say I'm a terminal man.'

'Well, let me tell you something Sammy, we're all terminals in here. Not one of us is walking out of this joint.'

Abul turned slowly to look at Stanley, his delicate wisps of hair quivering slightly in the dead air of the hospital room. He sucked in a shallow breath like it was all the effort in the world and asked, 'what about you?'

'Me? Well, you could say the big C got me too. Lung cancer.' Stanley cut off the end of the word cancer with a sharp 'a' to somehow emphasise its terminability.

'Started off as a little black spot on my lung but I guess it's spread damn near everywhere now.'

Stanley winced a little in pain and then hit the button on his PCA pump releasing another round of morphine into his fragile nervous system.

'You got a lot of pain Sammy?'

Abul shook his head.

'Not too bad pain.'

'Well that's one thing they're pretty good at round here - morphine. The food may be shit but they don't skimp on the drugs. If you want 'em, you can have 'em. That's what they do best, drugs. Oh, and yoga.' Stanley laughed to himself which set off a series of hacking coughs.

'I bet you already know how to do that, eh? Yoga?'

Abul arched his eyebrows again - body language that Stanley now recognised as more sensitive and informative than he initially thought.

'Should get yourself one of these babies,' continued Stanley patting his little pump box, 'you can have yourself real sweet dreams.' Stanley coughed again, hard and hacking this time, into his fist. He noticed a little blood on his hand and reached for a tissue to wipe it up.

'Damn it.'

'Are you alright?'

'Sure. Right as God-damn rain.'

The little brown man stared off into the distance.

'I have dreams alright' said Abul, 'I don't need any more dreams'.

'So, what's a guy like you dream about?'

Abul turned towards his roommate. His shrunken face had the look of a withered apple that had gone to seed.

'Bad things that have happened in my life,' said Abul.

'Oh yeah, like what?'

With what seemed like a Herculean effort, Abul hauled himself up into a sitting position and turned to face Stanley full on.

'May I ask your name?'

'Stanley.'

'Hello Stanley, my name is Abul Ibrahim Ahmed. Have you been here long?'

'Well, you could say I've been calling this hospital home for a quite a while now Sammy, yeah.'

'Please, if you don't mind, my name is Abul.'

'Alright then, Abul. So what about these dreams of yours.'

The door swung violently open and the two were interrupted by someone peering in at the doorway. It was Eddie from down the hall. Another patient. Ed was a wild-eyed man with an unshaven face, dishevelled hair and a sharp angular voice. He was leaning heavily on a hospital-issue aluminium-frame walker.

'Ya seen my tennis racket?'

Stanley turned and whispered to Abul, 'Eddie here thinks he's a tennis pro. Just play along.'

'Got a big game today - semi-finals ya know, me versus Sampras.'

'Is that right Ed? Haven't seen your racket anywhere in here, but if it shows up we'll be sure to give ya a holler. You keeping alright otherwise Ed?'

'Ah, damn it Stanley, how am I gonna win the grand slam without my lucky racket?'

'Ah, you'll find a way Ed - you always do.'

'Did you see me beat Connors at the French Open last week? That was a tight one I tell ya.'

The two men watched Eddie's wild eyes flash with excitement as the synapses in his brain fired off random images.

'Did ya see Connor's face at match point. Sonofabitch still thought he had a chance.'

'You had him all the way Ed. No contest.'

'Sonofabitch right. Gotta find that racket.'

'Hey Eddie, this here's a new fella, Abul, just joined us.'

'You seen my tennis racket Abul?'

'I am very sorry, no. Maybe you could give me a few pointers when you do, I was a keen player back in the day.'

Eddie stared blankly at the two of them for a long beat.

'Well, if it shows up - let me know huh? Catch youse later.'

Then Eddie spun around and aimed his walker back the way he came, and he was gone.

'Ed's a little mad alright, but he can sure play a damn fine game of checkers.'

The fading afternoon light slanted down through the blinds making little stripes and shapes appear on the whitewashed walls.

'You were saying about that dream of yours.'

'Yes, of course. I dream vividly about the man I killed.'

'Hold on,' said Stanley, 'thought you said this was real - these dreams?'

'Oh, very much real. I will tell you my story if you would like to hear it?'

Stanley leaned back into his pillow, 'it's all yours.'

'I was married for twenty-five years. We had no children. Sajida couldn't have any. She was a very much beautiful woman.'

'Yeah, we all got one of those, but I'm curious about the you killing someone part.'

'Of course. Please, I continue. My wife and I used to like to go for walks. High in the Nepalese mountains we would trek. Whenever we could. It was very much peaceful and quiet up there, a very glorious place. It was our anniversary. Twenty-five years we had built our lives together.'

'You still married?'

'No, no. Sajida is gone. I continue please. It was the best and worst of times. Marriages with no children can really test a relationship. But we were so happy to still be together. To celebrate our anniversary, we decided to make a very special trip. We planned to hike from Kathmandu to Nagarkot. There is an old temple there. Just ruins now. But it is a very sacred place. Very special. When we got there we planned to renew our vows before God. It was springtime; the rivers were high with flood waters. The blossoms had just begun. It was a perfect time to be in the mountains.'

'You camp your way across?'

'Sure. We had a guide. A young man called Nikesh. He had a young wife and small child. A son. He told us many stories of his life as we sat together in the evenings. He was a devout Muslim, a good man, a strong man, too. We only had the rudiments of equipment, but Nikesh was a very skilled guide.'

'So, what happened?'

'It was on our seventh day, Sajida was very tired, the terrain had been arduous, unforgiving. We had walked many hard miles that day. We decided to stop and found a place high above a gorge. We ate some rice and dried fruit and Nikesh made us some tea. Sajida looked so happy; I can still imagine her smiling face. She held a lifetime in those eyes, but she was still more beautiful than ever. We had finished eating. It was growing dark, and Sajida helped Nikesh clear the evening's dishes. The rest is almost like some awful dream. I still can't quite believe it. One minute I was admiring the two of them from a distance, making two perfect silhouettes against the reddening sky, then in the next heartbeat, they were gone.'

'Whaddayamean gone?'

'It must have been the rains that had loosened the earth, but the ground gave way and swallowed them up. They simply vanished. I ran to the edge and desperately looked for them. Down below, laid out on the rocks, I could just barely make out two figures. The night was closing in. Darkness comes very quickly in the mountains. I heard the voice of Nikesh calling for help, but there was nothing I could do. Not until morning. The climb down was too dangerous.'

The door opened again, and Nurse Norma noisily entered the room carrying a tray containing some vials and a syringe.

'You must be Abul,' said Norma as she double checked the chart. 'It's time to make you feel better. You feeling nauseous?'

Abul shook his head.

'Well good,' said Norma, 'looks like things are working then.'

Norma poked a needle into the little vial, measured up a small amount of antiemetic drug and proceeded to inject it into Kabul's main IV line.

'There. That should do it. Keep ya happy for a while. We don't want you boys getting uncomfortable on my watch.'

Norma made her way over to Stanley and lifted his head and rearranged his pillows, propping him upright.

'How about you Stanley? Everything alright? How's your pain today?'

'Good as can be expected Norma. My little friend here is keeping me happy.' Stanley gently patted his little blue box.

'Hey Norma, what haute cuisine can we expect tonight?'

'You boys could be in luck. Rumour has it that it's Italian night. Thank your lucky stars it's not that Mexican fiesta again. Mexican fiasco is what I say. Never seen so much food being chucked away. Think they'd have learned by now. They don't know when to leave good enough alone.'

'Do you think you might be able to sneak us in a nice little bottle of Chianti? Special treat, huh?'

Norma laughed her no-nonsense laugh.

'Would be nice wouldn't it, could go for a glass or two myself.' She leaned in close to Stanley and whispered, 'I have been known to turn a blind eye on occasion.' Norma pulled the curtains closed and straightened up the rest of the room.

'Alright fellas - seems my work here is done for the time being. Holler if you need anything.'

Abul appeared to have nodded off to sleep - the drug's side-effects taking immediate effect. In the darkening shadows of the room Stanley watched his new roommate breathing, the slight shallow breaths barely making an impact on his wasted body. His blankets made a smooth mound of a shape, and from where Stanley laid he looked like some kind of large fish. Stanley leaned back into his pillow and closed his eyes. He and a ten-year-old Brian were beachcombing along the deserted Oregon coast. The mist on the Pacific Rim was heavy and soupy and clung to the shoreline. As the two walked along, Brian combed the beach for any undiscovered treasures - agates that flashed brightly and stood out amongst the other ordinary stones in the hazy phosphorescent morning light. The sea lapped gently against the land, pulling and pushing like seasoned lovers. The air was bracing and pungent,
infused with the smells of salt and kelp. Brian spotted something and picked it up. He was surprised when he held it up to take a closer look. It was a beautiful agate that glistened and sparkled in an almost flawless shade of white and from every angle looked like a near-perfect heart shape. Brian called out for his Dad to come and have a look.

'Wow, Bri - that's amazing. A heart-shaped rock. That's good luck. Wait till Mom sees that beaut.'

'I'm gonna keep this one for sure. It's my favourite stone ever,' said Brian holding the precious find tightly in his hand.

Stanley looked out across the inlet. The water was like a mirror, as smooth as glass. About fifty yards away the water gently cut open as the dorsal fins of two great Orcas came up for air.

'Brian - quick look!'

'Where?'

'Right over there,' said Stanley pointing. The two waited with baited breath for what seemed like ages before the waters finally burst open again and a magnificent glossy black and white shape rose spectacularly up out into the air, made an arc, and then came crashing down into the cool clear brine with a great splash. Then all was quiet again; the inlet cloaked in its mysterious misty backdrop.

'Dad that was amazing! Think we'll see more?'

'Not sure Bri. Best keep your eyes peeled.'

Father and son stood side by side, quiet and meditative, both thinking their own thoughts.

'Well you don't see that every day, huh? Wanna keep going?'

Brian put his treasured stone into his pocket and the two continued meandering along the beach. When they rounded the bend they came to a standstill and stood dead in their tracks. Straight ahead of them, half in, and half out of the water was a stranded killer whale. Its shiny skin was dull and greyed and looked dried out and cracked. It looked like it had been there for some time and a group of gulls screeched and fought for picking rights at the large open gash in its side - a horrendous pink swath of ripped fat and fibre. Stanley and Brian approached tentatively while the gulls squawked their disapproval at them. The animal was enormous, much bigger up close. Brian fingered his prized stone for reassurance as it rubbed against his thigh. The closer they got they began to notice a smell. It was almost sickly sweet; the smell of decay, rot, and death. Brian picked up a stick lying nearby and bravely ventured closer to the beast. The Orca's open mouth, with its rounded teeth as white as Brian's rock, formed a strange half-smile that reminded him of the grinning painted faces of his sister's horse masks. Brian poked at the creature with his stick. The Orca's eye twitched and seemed to look straight at its unwitting perpetrator. Brian jumped back in horror and dropped his stick. The whale stared at Brian blankly, unwavering.

'It's OK Bri, it's dead. It's probably just a nerve impulse,' said Stanley.

'It's alive Dad, I know it is,' shrieked the shocked young boy, 'I don't like it.'

The Orca's eye glazed over again, satisfied to have looked upon the last of the indignities it would have to suffer here on earth, or perhaps just wanting to finish with the job at hand and die. Stanley took his son's hand.

'C'mon Brian, let's get back,' and the two turned and walked in silence away from the great beast. As they made the long trek Brian couldn't help but look back once or twice to make sure it hadn't moved or that it wasn't watching them. Steadily and surely the thing began to disappear into the mist. Before they rounded the final bend Brian took one last look, and now with such a distance between them, the whale just looked like some dark contour on the horizon. It could have been anything - a log, a tree stump, or some piece of debris washed up by an indiscriminate ocean, instead of a once magnificent animal in the throes of death.

Stanley awoke feeling tired and restless. It hadn't been a good night's sleep; he'd been feverish and had suffered drug-induced nightmares all night. He'd had to call for the nurse twice to bring him some Gravol and top up his morphine pump. Mornings are always the busiest time in hospitals; the hand-over from the night before, the changing of the guard. There are breakfasts to dole out, medications to give, bags of piss to change, and doctors starting to make their rounds, prioritising the patients into categories of 'fine', 'urgent' and 'do not resuscitate'.
Stanley didn't feel up to the yoga, he didn't feel up to too much to be honest. Abul was still asleep, his breath, no more than a slight wheeze. It looked like he had evaporated even more in the night. A disappearing man. Perhaps it was possible he was leaking out of all the tubes they'd stuck into him, thought Stanley. A nurse came and began the morning routine, hanging a new bag of saline, opening the curtains, and generally tidying up. Stanley couldn't face breakfast - a piece of dry toast and a plastic cup of canned fruit and could only manage to suck a little water through a straw. The nurse gently roused Abul

awake and the little brown man's bird eyes peeled open once more and began to take in the reality of another day.

'So, you never finished your story. I'm curious what happened next?'

Abul looked at Stanley, his eyebrows raised once again.

'Of course, you wish to know how I killed a man.'

Stanley opened his mouth to speak but Abul raised a withered, blue-veined hand to cease his efforts.

'It is alright. It is natural to want to know what it is like the moment when someone's life unnaturally ends. I will tell you.' Abul gazed off into the distance, remembering images in his mind's eye.

'The next morning, I climbed down to where my wife and Nikesh had fallen. It was very difficult. Very steep. It took me over an hour to reach them safely. It was clear that Sajida was dead. Mercifully she had died straight away; her head had hit a rock.'

'Holy shit. You must have been . . .'

'There are some things in life you can never prepare for; the birth of a child for instance, and the death of a loved one. It is true; my heart was never to be the same again. It was a great shock. But what could I do? It is one of the cruel facts of life, Stanley; the need to carry on when what you cherish has been taken from you.'

'What about Nikesh?'

'Nikesh was still alive. He was in very bad shape. His back was broken and he had many other injuries. There was no way he could be moved.'

Stanley watched Abul telling his tale, his small thin hands emphasising the details. They reminded Stanley of Ann's small hands. When she had had her second stroke he'd been out getting the shopping, running errands. She had lain on the bathroom floor motionless, barely alive for a long time before he found her. The paramedics arrived, revived her from death's door and she has remained an invalid ever since. Stanley wondered if it wouldn't have been better if she had died right then? Spare her the present indignities. What was the meaning of her life now? What was there left for her to do but merely survive?

Abul continued, 'for two nights I never left his side. We prayed together. He told me everything he wanted to say to his wife and son. I memorised those words like I was preparing for an exam. I didn't want to let him down. When he would sleep, I would work at burying my wife. There wasn't much around except for rocks and stones so I did what I could to preserve her dignity. Stone by stone, I covered her body. On the morning of the third day Nikesh was still conscious, but he looked bad. He was suffering tremendous pain, barely with it. I shared the last of my water with him.' Abul picked up his little plastic cup, took a sip and continued. 'It is against God's will to take another's life. But in my heart, I knew I had to help this man. I hoped that God would understand that he would have mercy on me. I took Nikesh's knife from his holster. I made a prayer the end would be swift and certain. Then I pushed the blade deep into his heart. His suffering ended then.'

Abul closed his eyes and made a praying gesture with his hands. Stanley had never met anyone who had killed someone before. He wondered if he'd have had the courage to do such a thing if it had been him. Who knows what you're capable of when pushed to the edges of what life can throw at you? But instead, here he was, listening to another man's tragic story. A disappearing man facing his own uncertain ending. And hoping that, it too, would be merciful.

Abul slept through most of the day. In and out of consciousness as the drugs and his expiring body ebbed and flowed like the tide.

Awake. Asleep. Aware. Adrift.

Here and then gone. On the precipice. A tug of war. Life and death both vying for dominance. Norma quietly came and went, sensing what she had witnessed so many times before coming to its natural conclusion. She made sure that Abul remained comfortable and checked his vitals hourly. In the early evening Abul woke up and seemed to muster a second wind.

'You know that was quite some story you told there', said Stanley, 'guess you can't judge a book by its cover. You can never guess what's inside a man's head.'

'Or inside his heart' wheezed Abul. 'We can only do that which we are capable of. Nothing more.'

'You ever tasted bourbon Abul?'

Abul looked at Stanley and shook his head.

'I do not drink. It is forbidden in my religion.'

'Well, I don't think there is much more you could do to piss God off, not after what you told me today, but I've got a little bit of living still to do and I'll be damned, I ain't gonna go out with any regrets.'

Stanley poured himself a little jig of bourbon into his hospital-issue plastic cup and took a small drink. The rough velvet liquid fell down the back of his throat with a warming pleasure. Abul watching Stanley drink his whiskey with a curiosity.

'You know Stanley, I often think about regrets. But what should we do with them at this point of our lives? When it is too late to do anything. Should I regret killing Nikesh? Should I regret taking Sajida hiking in the mountains? Should I regret the love I felt only to discover the same depths of grief when she died? To deny one is to deny both.'

'Never really thought of it that way,' said Stanley taking another sip of bourbon.

'There is one thing that I do regret,' said Abul.

'What's that?'

'I never learned how to smoke.'

Stanley almost spit out his drink in surprise.

'No shit. You killed a man, buried your wife with your bare hands, but that's your big regret? Not smoking?'

Abul smiled at Stanley.

'As a young boy in India my father and I would watch films at the local cinema. I loved the American Westerns. Every Saturday we would go together. My mother would pack us one samosa each and some rose water tea. Clint Eastwood was my favourite. He was the coolest. I always wanted to be a cowboy just like him. Wear a big hat. Ride into the sunset smoking an American cigarette. For a couple of hours each week I would be transported out of my own life, out of my poor existence, out of India. It was magical. Those are my fondest memories of childhood.'

'Hey,' said Stanley, 'Fist Full of Dollars - it doesn't get much better. I don't think there is a man alive wouldn't want what Clint had. Well, you know what he would say? What's a shot of cowboy whiskey without a smoke? It's like salt and pepper, coffee and cream. Somethings are just meant to be together. And we just happen to have the supplies with us here tonight, what do you say Abul - no regrets?'

Stanley poured another little beaker full of whiskey and passed it to Abul.

'That there is Tennessee fire water. The real cowboy shit.'

He took out two Marlboro's from the pack in his drawer and lit them both, passed one to Abul and once again he filled his own fragile lungs with the warm nicotine filled smoke and held his breath. He felt a warm pleasure as the nicotine infused into his body's struggling cells.

'Cheers my friend, here's to that bucket list of yours.' Stanley exhaled and let out a deep ragged cough.

'Geez, maybe that's helping to clear things up,' and the two laughed out loud.

Abul tentatively put the cigarette into his mouth and inhaled.

'Take it slow now partner, you don't want to get a head rush' warned Stanley.

Abul exhaled a long stream of blue smoke into the stale hospital air and closed his eyes to focus on the sensation that was engulfing his body. He took a drink of bourbon and raised his cup to Stanley,

'To Clint'.

'To cowboys, new and old,' said Stanley.

'Now I am, how you say, a badass,' said Abul and the two laughed again.

'So, tell me Stanley, what is the most badass thing you've ever done in your life?'

'Geez Louise, where to start? I never killed no one, but I'm sure I got a list of offences as long as my arm. Cheating on my taxes maybe? Nah, every sonofabitch does that.'

Stanley looked at the cigarette between his fingers and thought about things for a moment.

'You know there was one thing that sure seemed pretty damn funny at the time. I used to work in a restaurant when I was at university. Back in my good old rebellious days. Pretty upscale joint too, fancy food, wine lists and all that. Had this real prick of a manager. Jonathan Wright. Can still picture his smug little face. Self-righteous little weasel, used to lord it over us all the time. Have you ever worked in a restaurant Abul?'

Abul shook his head and took another drag of his cigarette.

'Well, let's just say you earn every damn penny. We're talking sweat and blood. It would be a right panic some nights. I ain't kidding. Proper manic. Anyway, point is we all worked our doggies off - except for John-boy who just used to stand at the front door and greet people. Come to think of it, guy even looked like a weasel. At the end of the shift, we'd all gather round and shoot the shit. It was the nightly ritual. Shoot the shit and enjoy a deserving smoke. Well Johnny-boy would join us, just like he was one of the gang see. And every night the little prick would help himself to a nice cold beer. On the house, manager's privilege. And he would just stand there drinking that lovely cold one right in front of us poor parched bastards. Never once offered us a drink. We all hated him for that. So one night Jonathan gets a phone call, takes it in the other room. Anyway, I notice he's left his beer sitting on the table so I grab it, pull out my dick and piss a little into it.'

Abul chuckled, 'No?!'

'Just a little bit. But I gotta tell you the satisfaction we all felt when the bastard came back and took that next swig. He didn't notice anything different. But we all knew.'

'Stanley, you are indeed one badass dude!'

'Yeah, well coulda got myself fired for that stunt, but it was well worth it. Just to see that smug bastard's face sipping on my piss.'

The door opened and in stepped Norma.

'Well, well, I leave you guys alone for five minutes and what do you two get up to - smoking! Sorry fellas, you know what I'm gonna say don't ya? Geez and are you hitting the bottle too? Stanley! Is this your bad influence on poor Mr. Ahmed?'

'Ah c'mon Norma, not like it's gonna kill anyone.'

'Excuse me mister, what about us hired help? Ain't you ever heard about second-hand smoke? Anyway, you know what'll happen if I allow it? They'll have my scalp, never mind give me a disciplinary. So, if y'all be so kind, recess is over boys.'

Abul took a final puff on his first and only cigarette and passed the half-finished butt to Norma.

'Thank you, Norma, for letting my friend show me how to be a real cowboy.'

'An Indian cowboy huh? Well now I've heard everything. Alrighty boys, keep the drinking to yourselves. But no more smoking in here alright?"

Abul leaned his head back onto his pillow, his eyebrows happily raised and a small, contented smile spread across his withered face.

The man with no name, Mexican poncho casually thrown over his shoulder, hat dipped below one eye, turned his horse to face the red-glowing Arizona sun setting in the west. He looked out across the vast landscape, the rugged red-rock canyons to the East and the river valley to the west. He took one last drag of the cigarette and flicked it onto the parched desert ground. He took his rifle out of its holster and laid it across his lap. The cowboy moved his trusty steed forwards, heading towards the setting sun. As the words 'The End' scrolled across the cinematic screen, his silhouette began to slowly disappear into the horizon.

Abul never woke up again. At four am, Stanley opened his weary eyes and watched as two porters, dressed in pressed hospital whites, quietly and swiftly moved the body out of the room. When Stanley finally woke up proper it was well past nine o'clock and the room was half empty again. Everything was the same, yet everything had changed. A new nurse was busy with the morning routine. A tray of hospital food stood nearby on a plastic tray. Untouched. Stanley was feeling lousy, not so much because of the drinking and smoking, but because his cancer was steadily eating away at every part of him now, advancing cell by cell, winning the battle and shutting down organs.

Stanley made his way to the commode and felt his woozy stomach churn over. He threw up into the toilet bowl - a horrid yellow coloured liquid. Bile. He vomited twice more draining his stomach of its contents. He was so ragged and wretched. He barely managed to sit himself down on the toilet seat. He felt like death warmed over. He caught his reflection in the bathroom mirror. He looked damn awful. Drawn. Pale. Scruffy. How long had it been since he had last shaved? Must have been a few days. A week? He suddenly felt the need to make his appearance right. Tidy himself up. All his life he had hated to look unkempt. It was one of Stanley's quirks. Even on the camping trips he'd always made it his thing to stay clean shaven. Never mind being outdoorsy and rustic he just hated that feeling of itchy stubble. On occasions he'd shaven in frigid mountain streams, or in salty ocean rock pools, anything but look untidy. Mostly he would just boil a little water on the Coleman, pull out his little traveling kit and shave using the wing mirrors of the van. With all the strength he could muster Stanley ran some water into the basin and soaped up his face. He was shaky and weak with a bone weariness he'd never felt before in his life. It was like every fibre and cell in his body had turned against him. He was feeling the desperate need to crawl back into bed and hit the morphine button a thousand times. But Stanley was determined. He carefully lifted the blade to his face and scraped away the grey hairs and then rinsed himself clean. It was all he had left. He managed the few steps back to his bed and crawled under the covers. He was sweating and cold. A fever was racing through his system. His body was a raging battlefield.

He glanced once more around the whitewashed room. The morning light was weakly streaming through the window, giving the room a gauzy angelic haze. His half-empty pack of Marlboros sat on the table beside the Beanie Baby. A plastic water cup, the TV remote and a framed picture of Ann sat nearby. Stanley hit his morphine button, quietly closed his eyes, and soon drifted off into a sea of drug-induced visions and memories.

The rain fell in a fine steady mist. The sky hung down low and seemed to kiss the ground in places. The Pacific Ocean was calm and ebbed and flowed, gently tossing and turning the pebbles on the shore. It would take a millennia before they would be perfectly smooth and another millennia before they would be ground down into sand. The morning was still and quiet. A pup tent stood next to a small fire pit. A few embers of wood still smouldered, slowly surrendering to the ceaseless Oregon downfall. A single swirl of smoke drifted aimlessly upward attempting to reach the heavy sky. A man sat cross-legged on a large boulder and gazed out across the endless horizon. The rain had an undisputed beauty all its own and painted the scene in a distinctive West Coast panorama. Slowly he climbed down and walked along the beach. He slipped off his running shoes and left them by the water's edge. The sea felt cold but refreshing against his toes, ankles, calves. He waded out deeper, up to his knees, his thighs. The water was crystal clear, and he could see everything that lay on the ocean floor around him. A starfish. A small crab making its way across the seabed. A garden of kelp. Through the shimmering waters he caught sight of a magnificent white stone. The stone made the shape of a perfect heart and glowed with a whiteness that was breathtaking. He reached down to fetch it. Sea water dripped down his elbows as he held it up into the morning light. It wasn't a stone. It was a tooth. A large, polished Orca tooth.

The underwater world was magnificent. The ocean bed was a fantastic landscape of vibrant colours and textures. Creatures of all shapes and sizes meandered freely along its rocky depths. Deep water currents pulled and tugged at seaweed arms that waved and swayed as tiny fish darted this way and that. The black and white Orca appeared out of the depths. She was an animal of such grace and beauty. Instinctive and free to roam. She swam up from the depths, broke the surface and lurched up into the air and rain. The great splash echoed across the inlet. The Orca dived down and traced the contour of the shore as if to survey the land it kissed. She turned herself to face the deeper waters of the open sea and sprayed a long watery breath out of her spout into the moist autumnal air. It would be some time before she returned to these deep clear waters. Everything would be different, and nothing would have changed. The glistening stones that lay strewn along the shoreline would still be tossed and turned by wave upon wave. Always in the process of becoming, they would continue to be gently shaped and rounded into perfection through an unhurried evolution, while nearby on the sandy shore the footprints of a disappearing man had already dissolved back into the landscape.

Sticks and Stones

'Tiffany and Brad' I announced, confident I had made the perfect choice of names for the twenty-something couple just walking past.

'Nah, too suburban, too eighties . . . more like an Ashley and . . .' he squinted his eyes slightly, like he always did when he was scanning his brain's computer files, searching for the perfect name. 'Carter', he sneered with confidence, 'Ashley and Carter'.

The young couple passed in front of the diner window and stopped for a moment to look inside.

'They look like a walking advertisement for Tommy Hilfiger' I added. 'Oh my God, I think they're coming in,' I said, averting my eyes guiltily down towards the floor.

'No way' he assured, 'there's a Starbucks just down the street, and they are so fucking Starbucks'.

I giggled, 'you are good'. I reached into my faux leopard thrift-store purse for my cigarettes and offered him the pack, 'Smoke?'

'Yeah, thanks.' He pulled out two, and with John Travolta coolness, put them both in his mouth and lit them with his Harley Davidson Zippo lighter. He exhaled and handed one to me.

'It's a gift you know', he said only half joking, his dark eyes squinting again, this time, in self-satisfaction. I took a long drag, elegantly leaned my arm on the arborite tabletop and coolly blew smoke rings towards the window. I cradled the cigarette sensually between my long white fingers, showing off my freshly painted black nails, in what was my best attempt to evoke a film-noir-gothic-girl look.

'Oh, this will be good', I said, spying the next unsuspecting victims, 'let's see, hmmm . . . Charles and Miriam, no wait . . . Penelope. Charles and Penelope'.

Putting on a supercilious accent he added, 'Charles is a senior partner in an accounting firm, still has his English accent after all these years, loves lawn bowling and has a penchant for stamp collecting.'

I continued, 'Penelope belongs to a book club, adores miniature poodles and hasn't had a decent orgasm since nineteen-seventy-three.'

He grinned and picked out the next unsuspecting victims, 'wait, here comes Brian and Kevin.' Then putting on a lisp he continued, 'they've been in a civil partnership for several years now. Brian, the one wearing the spray-on pants, wants to go all the way, get married and raise a couple of Chihuahuas but Kevin has been secretly screwing another waiter, Demetrius, from the Greek Taverna, La Costas, where he works.'

Without missing a beat I continued, 'oh, look it's Elliot and Phoebe the perfect picture of yuppiedom just parking the family Beemer, accompanied by their three well-adjusted and spoiled brat heirs . . .'

He picked it up and effortlessly added, 'Dylan, Quentin and Madison.'

We both burst out laughing.

A frumpy middle-aged waitress arrived at our table toting a coffeepot, 'coffeth? she lisped, the remnant of a childhood harelip still present in her now ageing voice.

'Sure . . . Melody', he said reading the waitress' plastic name-tag out loud, 'that'd be great, top us up.'

'Sure doesn't seem like a Melody to me,' I whispered after the waitress had gone, 'more of a Marjorie, or a Wilma.'

'Awe c'mon, maybe she's just plain old harelip-Mary. Maybe you should saunter over there and tell her she needs to change her name; 'Harelip Mary' from now on, cause we, in booth five, decided so!'

'Oh God, she's probably been working in this dump forever,' I said, surveying the surroundings and cringing at the thought.

I looked into his angular face, those dark bedroom eyes, that mischievous grin, that perfect stubble. With his ubiquitous leather biker jacket and jet-black pompadour, he was the height of retro-fifties cool. We'd only known each other for a few months, since the Fall semester started. I was an English Lit Major and he was a floundering Liberal Arts student. We were in a Creative Writing class together; that's where we met. Like two stranded outcasts finding each other in a sea of archaic academia, we quickly discovered we shared the same caustic wit, disdain of mundane normalcy, and so we sorta glommed on to each other and started hanging out. He'd come over sometimes with some cheap wine, or fightin' sherry, as he called it, and we'd order pizza and watch old movies. I caught his rockabilly band, *The Rattlesnake Jakes*, a few times at the student union pub nights; they're really good, high energy. He plays standup bass in the band. He said he named his bass Stella, after the Streetcar Named Desire character, because she puts up with a lot of abuse. But his real passion is avoiding responsibility. A rebellion that stems from his middle-class upbringing, an uptight banker father, upwardly mobile older siblings and a mother that avoids reality through a daily ritual of vodka tonics: the classic dysfunctional modern family. University is more of a place to avoid reality than a serious proposition for him, a chance to access the family educational trust fund. Sure beats real work, he says. But underneath his rebellious facade he's a really smart guy, even if he doesn't apply himself much. He reads a lot and he turned me onto Kerouac and Bukowski, a liberation from all those dreary romance poets we have to study in Lit class. He's got a real natural way with writing too, when he puts his mind to it. As for me, I'll probably just finish my degree and by the time I'm thirty, be leading some tragic Sylvia Plath-like existence, writing my dark little poetry and working as an editor someplace.

'You know I was reading the other day that in some native cultures they believe in changing your name several times in a life. Kinda like shedding your skin. They believe that one name won't fit you for your whole life, you need a few, according to the article.'

'Really?' he said, sounding dubious.

'Once you outgrow a name you choose a new one, one that represents the new you. . . y'know, like the next phase of your life. Sounds kinda cool, huh? Then they have a big tribal celebration in your honour. Like a coming-out party.'

'No shit? Well, who are you gonna be next then?'

I shrugged and took another long drag and concentrated on making the perfect smoke ring curl up the windowpane. Before I could say anything, he blurted out,

'I got it - Suzi . . .Suzi with a fuckin'Z.'

'Suzi?' I replied indignantly, 'I don't think . . .'

'Yeah, Suzi Cyanide! What a great fucking stage name! You could come and sing with the band - *Suzi Cyanide and the Rattlesnake Jakes*! That sounds fuckin' brilliant!' He started drumming on the table and singing a classic Robert Gordon song, 'my gal is red hot, your gal ain't doodly squat.'

'Jesus, you know I can't sing, besides, if I was the singer what would what's-his-face . . . Billy, do?'

'Ah, Bill's being a real asshole lately, c'mon it'd be a real gas.'

'Get real! Besides I really hate the name Suzi, I always have. Sue, Susan . . . they all sound so little-girlish. Jesus, I'd have to start wearing mohair sweaters and everything.'

He looked at me momentarily dejected, stubbed out his cigarette and stared off into space.

'Hey, how's your story coming?' I said, deftly trying to change the subject.

'I dunno,' he shrugged.

'Well, what's it about?'

'Ah ya know, just some shit I made up.

'Yeah, but what is the shit all about,' I asked, trying to sound encouraging. He straightened himself up and poured three packets of sugar into his coffee.

'You know we were supposed to write a character thing, right?' I nodded in agreement. 'Well, I'm doing this piece about a nerdy kid who wants to be a rock star. It's a fucking diatribe, a satirical look at the trials and tribulations of trying to get laid.'

'Is it about screwing or rock and roll?' I laughed.

'Oh, there's a difference,' he spat back. 'It's supposed to be funny, y'know, black humour, sex and drugs and rock 'n roll. The main character's this real geeky kid, Orville, he worships the band Devo, remember them – ARE WE NOT MEN?'

'I love that song, it's so eighties.'

'Right, so this kid represents all the losers, geeks and nerds – I mean you can't get more geeky than Devo, right?'

'Sounds funny - love to read it sometime.'

'You wanna hear some of it now?' he asked, suddenly brightening up.

'Sure.' I said, stubbing out my cigarette and reaching for another. He rummaged around in his bag and pulled out a pile of crumpled papers.

'Okay,' he said, setting up the story. 'Som this kid is a total maniac for all things Devo, right? I mean, we're talking totally obsessed. So, he's wearing this dumb Devo costume to school in honour of their newly released single, *Whip it*, ya know, the toxic suit, the plastic wig, the glasses, the whole nine yards.'

'Yeah, I remember you could order that stuff off the back of their albums – total geekdom.'

'Exactly. Anyhow, it's lunchtime and Orville stumbles into a room full of football jerks.'

The cafeteria was full of jocks and their dumb cheerleader girlfriends. I'd just got some fries and a black cherry yogurt when some pigskin-throwing ape decided to trip me in front of all his friends. Funny fucking joke! My tray flipped up and fries and yogurt flew everywhere. My face ended up between the tits of Tarzan's nubile girlfriend. She giggled, and I remember thinking that a perfectly fine pair of female ornaments were being wasted on a two-stroke, Camaro-driving clown like this. God, I decided, had the same sense of humour as me. I stood up and began wiping cherry yogurt off my Devo wig. Then came the insult - hey dickhead, why don't you WHIP IT out and give us all a laugh? Now moronic insults I could take, but no one, NO ONE, makes fun of Devo! The blood pounded in my temples and I straightened my wig in readiness for battle. I swung the empty tray round, like an oversize Frisbee, smashing it into Tarzan's Neanderthal brow. Leaping across the table, I grabbed a fork and lunged with lethal force at the enemy's jugular. The primal beat of Devo music played in my mind as I worked with Ninja dexterity forcing one eye free from its socket of the surprised, dumbstruck linebacker. The nubile screamed in terror and awe. Sunlight glinted off the menacing, blood-drenched fork. 'Are we not men?' begged the response, 'WE ARE FUCKING DEVO!' at 100 decibels in my head. I was on a mission for all the nerds, creeps, chess-club and stage-band members, debating-team-average-fucking-Joes that never get to fuck cheerleaders in the backseats of Mom and Dad's BMW. This was beyond Devo; this was us against them. I grabbed a handful of T-shirt between the nubile's tits, snapping her bra off with primordial skill. I slung the brassiere round Tarzan's neck like a lasso and pulled tightly, fastening the titty tourniquet into his scalp with the bloody fork.

His hand went up and caught me under the chin. I bit down hard, severing his finger clean off. He dropped the hold like a high-school football team fumble on the ten-yard line. Crowds of pimply faces gathered round. Black cherry yogurt and sweat trickled down the Devo wig as my temples pounded like drums. Young girls started gathering round in disbelief and intrigue, staring at me, their panties getting wet at the sight of this new teen-age action hero. I could already envision a threesome fuck-a-thon later with two virginal grade niners, to the strains of Devo's classic Stone's re-make of 'Satisfaction'. Satisfaction, unlike Mr. Jagger's experience, would be had by all. I was about to deal the final crushing blow when the lunch bell rang. A hand grabbed me by the shoulder - Principal Jones. The fight was over. Kids scurried back to science labs, French classes and gym-room lockers. Word of my heroic deeds would spread like wildfire. The football team would be missing a linebacker in the next game. I would get expelled. Devo would be proud.

He put the papers down and looked expectantly up at me.

'Well, what do you think?'

I hesitated, 'it's good, funny . . . a bit over the top . . .but funny y'know?'

'You don't like it? You think it's stupid.' He scooped up the papers and started cramming them back into his bag.

'No, it's good, really . . .it's just that, well, what I mean is . . . look, do you really want me to be honest?'

'Abso-fuckin-lutely,' he nodded.

'Well, it seems a little a bit misogynous you know?'

'What the hell does that mean?'

'Well, it means that it would probably be a little offensive to most women. I mean it's fine, it's just totally written from a typical male point of view that's all.'

'I think you've missed the fucking point' he spat back, obviously hurt by my frankness.

'I don't know, it's just . . .' the words faded into an awkward silence that threatened to engulf us. Damn it, he was so good at making those puppy-dog eyes, 'hey, what the hell do I know anyway?' I backpedalled, 'it made me laugh! And I love the symbolic use of Devo, that was cool; I mean, like you totally captured that devolution of man thing, back to his primordial caveman instincts.'

But it was too late; he stared blankly at me, more hurt than angry.

'Got another smoke?' he asked, sounding detached.

'Hey, you know what we should do this afternoon?' I said, trying desperately to lighten up the atmosphere, 'dye each other's hair!' I hated awkwardness, and even if he was the one acting like a jerk right now, I wasn't gonna sit here and let it become a big deal. 'You would look so awesome platinum blond, just like Billy Idol!'

'I fucking hate Billy Idol,' he muttered under his breath. I followed his stare out the diner window and zoned in on another unwitting caricature walking past.

'Hey look, there's a Helen if ever there was,' I said, trying to steer us back to some sarcastic fun and lighten the mood up.

'Helen.'

He said the word so softly I almost didn't make it out. 'Helen,' he repeated, 'I knew a Helen once . . . she died,' his voice, a gentle wave of emotion.

'Really?' I mused.

'Yeah, we used to go out back in high school. She was smart, real smart, and beautiful too. Said she was gonna be an actress, move to New York, wanted to work in theatre, tread the boards on Broadway. Real acting she always called it. She wanted to do so many things . . .' his voice trailed off.

'She had a little brother, Maurice, used to get called Mo all the time. He was a Down Syndrome kid, sweetest kid you'd ever meet, a real character too. Shit, I remember this one time we took Mo with us for a picnic to the beach, just the three of us. Helen and I went in for a swim, when we got back, Mo had taken all the food and fed it to the gulls. Fucking gulls ate everything! He just sat there in the sand smiling his ass off, you couldn't even be mad at the little fucker. Helen more or less took care of him most of the time. She was so patient and kind. Her parents worked shifts, so she was always the one cooking the dinners for her and Mo and getting him ready for school and shit.'

'What happened to her?' I asked.

'Fire,' he said blankly. 'Wiped them out just like that' he said snapping his fingers. 'It happened early one December morning, about 4:00 am, no one had a chance, everyone was still sleeping. Whole house went up just like a haystack,' he said.

'No shit, how awful!' I said.

'They think it was Mo playing with the Christmas lights that started it. Some fucking Christmas lights that year! When they finally got Helen out, she had third degree burns over ninety percent of her body. They never got Mo out alive . . . the father was the only one; he was on night shift that week, missed the whole damn thing.'

'Jesus!'

'I went to see her in the hospital. You ever seen anyone burnt to a crisp?'

I shook my head sadly.

'Hardly recognised her. Didn't even look like a real person lying there. All these machines and shit plugged in, keeping her alive I guess.' He leaned forward, 'so I'm sitting there just shooting the shit ya know, didn't really know what the fuck to say, when this big mama of a nurse comes in - 'hi I'm Doreen' she says, 'Helen's nurse. I'm sorry but visiting hours are over, you'll have to leave now.' So, I'm just saying goodbye, when I feel Helen's fingers gently squeezing my hand. Jesus, I think, she's trying to tell me something! So, I lean in close, put my ear over her mouth. What is it, Helen? I ask softly. Then I hear it.'

'Hear what, what did you hear?' I ask imploringly.

'Helen's last words before she died.'

'Jesus. No way. What did she say?' I asked, choking back the tears, 'What was it?'

'In this hoarse little burnt-up voice she whispered to me . . . sure doesn't seem like a Doreen, does she?'

I looked at him, that mischievous grin just starting to spread across his face.

'You bastard', I said. 'You Goddamn bastard.'

Miss Information

It took willpower not to eat the lunch put in front of me. I was starving. But I knew what would happen if I did. Drugged. Poisoned. I took a mouthful and chewed obediently but then spat it out when they weren't looking. You had to be sharp, on guard all the time, stay one step ahead. The most important thing I was taught in training was to stay focused. If you didn't it was game over. I'm sure they were bemused by my appearance though. Transgendered people always come off a little strange, don't they? C'mon, I'm the first to admit it. I look at myself everyday, who's kidding who? Inside I may feel like I've finally put the biology to right, left behind those troubled years of confusion, misery, and doubt. But the world saw things differently - a she-male. I was always envious of the Ladyboys of Thailand. There was a femininity about them that seemed authentic. Plus they looked fantastic.

They carried it off in a way that none of us Western trans gals could. Sure, I could doll myself up, do my hair, put on make-up, hold myself, walk, talk, and behave like the woman I knew I was inside. But my hands always gave me away. Men's hands. To most of the world it still seemed so weird - a woman in a man's body literally begs attention, but it actually worked in my favour. C'mon, no one would really expect a tranny to be a spy.

Working for MI6 was something I more or less just fell into. It's not like you see a job posting down at the local jobcentre - 'spy wanted - apply within'. No, I was groomed for it. It was Gerald who mentored me - the love of my life. He had been part of MI6 for decades, a real pro, and a real gentleman too. Sure knew how to treat a lady. The first time anyone bought me flowers, it was Gerald. Sure, he had a wife and kids, lived a pedestrian life on the outside, but I didn't mind all that. When it came to his deepest desires - I was the one. We had a flare and passion that could light up the world. We were secret lovers for several years, until he got sick. Properly sick. Then he had to quit working, hang up his gun, retreat to convalesce at home. Back to the normal. We didn't see each other for a long time then. That was hard. His wife, Julia, taking charge, nursing him, mothering him, in what time he had left. Months, as it turned out. I'm sure it brought them closer, he had always loved her in his way. No nonsense Julia. It's just that, well you could say he was more complex, had more layers to him than his outward appearance allowed. Sure he loved her and the kids, but he kept secrets from them he could never reveal. I mean, I'd be hard to explain to anyone, never mind your own family. I never got to share our news with him though. It hadn't been confirmed before he died. I only managed an awful, gut-wrenching and rushed goodbye.

When he got sick and then died so quickly it took everyone by surprise. He was such a strong man. Only in his 50s. But that's what a life of smoking and drinking will get you - the downside of being a real-life James Bond. It had been a while since I'd seen him. We'd both been away on different missions, him in the Middle East and me in South America. It took a while before I found out. I mean it wasn't that unusual to be out of contact when you were deep inside an assignment. I would usually receive one of his coded messages though, nothing communicable, just some mumbo jumbo, but something that indicated everything was alright. It's funny how a meaningless text can mean so much, but I hadn't gotten anything from him in months. I called HQ. They told me the truth. Gerald was ill. Terminal. I was devastated.

We could never really be a couple out in public. That was clear from the start. I didn't mind, life was complicated enough without making it more so. I just relished the times we did have together. The romantic evenings in Knightsbridge. The weekends in Brighton. The getaways in the south of France when we could not give a damn about the stares, be a proper couple, gaze out across the Mediterranean, the balmy air making us light-headed and giddy. He would hold me in his strong arms, stroke my hair, share his cigarillo and delight me with stories about his exciting world of espionage.

There had been a time when we had talked about the possibility of him leaving his wife. But it was a fleeting notion at best. I think we both recognised the futility of that. No, I would remain his mistress. But that actually spiced things up, seeing each other like that, it was something we both longed for. Longing - it's good for the heart. I think Gerald saw me as somewhat of a kindred spirit - neither of us was what we appeared to be. Carrying that around with you all the time can be a tremendous burden, not something that most people can understand, but it brought us closer. At the funeral I stood in the back, kept a low profile, I didn't want to make any trouble for the family. They had enough on their plate. It was strange to see him eulogised as someone I barely recognized though. A father. A husband. A neighbour. Gerald. My Gerald. But not. I keep the tear I shed in church that day in a little vial. My own eulogy to him. May you rest in peace my love.

Before becoming Yvonne, I had been a highly trained soldier. A commando. I had served two terms in Afghanistan - Gerald saw my potential right away. Don't laugh; you'd be shocked at the number of servicemen who choose the army because of their mixed-up sexual feelings. As if embracing a full-on masculine role will keep the wolves at bay, disciplining yourself against your guilt-ridden thoughts will somehow make them go away. You wish. Yeah, I knew what discipline meant. I knew how to follow orders, run an outfit, drill the squadron. I also knew how to do my nails, shave my legs and how to pleasure a man. I had a longing to embrace my true nature. I lived with it every day. I hated army life, being a manly man. I loathed my masculinity like a curse. My big hands. But Gerald never made me feel that way. He only made me feel wanted, loved. Eventually I embraced a new life, as Yvonne DeCarlo.

'Not hungry today, Yvonne?'

The young black woman picked up my lunch plate and put it on the trolley with the others. I knew this ploy; I'd been down this road before.

'Play the game Yvonne'. I smiled vacantly and didn't say a word. She gave me a baleful look and then trundled away with her cart. I was in a mental health halfway house. But not a real one, this was just their front - I had them sussed. What they didn't know was that I was gathering information, collecting data. As long as I kept my head down, I'd soon have everything sorted.

Next they would come around with the medications. That was the routine, lunch, then meds. Truth serum passed off as something benign. This was trickier - how to pretend to swallow your meds. Thing was to keep it between the molars and the cheek - easy when you knew how. Then cough them up when you had the chance, keep the drugs hidden in your purse. Funny, they never checked there? Then later would come the questioning guised as therapy. This was where my abilities really shined. The delicate balance between making them think the serum had worked and feeding them duds. The answers had to appear natural, believable. But a life of pretending to be something you're not, had prepared me for this. Misinformation. It's funny now to think that's what Gerald used to call me, his affectionate nickname - his little 'Miss Information'.

Every time he gently slipped off my panties and acted shocked at the little surprise package there.

I hadn't heard from headquarters in a while, I needed to connect soon. I picked up my purse and played at putting on lipstick. Natural for a tranny girl to be constantly worrying about her appearance. But my compact held a two-way transmitter. Smart technology. I checked for a message but damn, still nothing. Never mind, a little powder for the nose, check my look. The nurse came along on cue and passed me the little paper cup of drugs. I threw back my head to indicate a good swallow, and off she went, satisfied. Soon as I could, I spat them out.

I was beginning to feel nervous. I would normally have had some word by now. I was thinking this was going to require another tact. A plan. I had no choice but to act alone, I couldn't stay here much longer. The notion of an escape plan started to take shape in my mind, and it would definitely require a little drama. Self-harming – that would work a treat. Something that would require medical treatment, get me out of here and sequestered in a hospital ward. There I'd have a chance. OK, now I had a plan.

I went into the bathroom and locked the door. I began to calmly cut my arm with a razor. Lots of little slashes, not too deep, but deep enough to draw blood. Quite a lot of blood. That's good, blood creates drama. A few smears across the face for added emphasis. Then the kicking and screaming. Breaking things. Anger. Hysterics. Picture this - a hysterical she-male in a fit of self-loathing, slashing away at her ugliness and imperfection. What a perfect foil. The whole team came to the rescue. I was restrained, sedated, bandaged, and quickly shipped off for medical attention. A 'cry for help' that would require treatment. I knew the drill. Psychiatrists. The prodding and poking into the disturbed subconscious. Oh, they'd have fun unravelling my subconscious all right! There would be a protocol, a treatment package. That would start tomorrow, but for now, the night had become quiet. Staff returned to their stations. The plan was working. As I lay in my hospital bed still woozy from the tranquilliser, I noticed I had a message. Finally, contact. I didn't want to take any chances, so I nonchalantly powdered my face, hit play, but it was garbled. Damn it. It must be poor reception in here or the bastards had descramble filters on. Still, it was contact at least, HQ was on it. I sent a message back to acknowledge, but it was looking like escape may be more difficult than I'd initially anticipated. For the moment there was nothing more to be done, escaping would have to wait. I fell back into a dreamy state of drugged consciousness and thought to myself, 'tomorrow always brings another chance to die another day.' That was one of Gerald's sayings. He used to quote lines from Bond films all the time. God, how I missed him.

I had always planned on going all the way with my transgender treatments. I had been taking hormone therapy for five years. Over time I had lost most of my body hair, and small feminine breasts had started to grow. I loved the presence of my new acquisitions, their smooth round undulations, and wearing a bra - I liked that too, a daily reminder of my burgeoning womanhood. I'd lost some of my muscle mass, too, giving me a gentler shape. Not exactly the curves of a woman, but less soldier-like now. The final step would be the surgery. Cutting off the penis to fashion a realistic vagina out of the unwanted flesh. There was something powerfully symbolic about losing that totemic appendage - completion. But you had to be 100% committed to this irreversible act, once the knife cuts there's no turning back. But I was more than ready. With the hormone treatments my penis had become quite small and ineffectual anyway, I rarely got an erection anymore. When the time came, Gerald saw me through the entire thing, holding my hand, bringing me flowers and girlie magazines to take my mind off things. He was always supportive, always loving. And then there I was. No longer his Miss Information.

This was the second of two surgeries I went through in a short space of time. The first one had been a little trickier, a clinical trial, highly experimental. A secret clinic in Switzerland. Organised through the top contacts of MI-6. The first time this type of procedure had ever been attempted on anyone, never mind a Tranny. A womb transplant.

The sedation drugs were starting to wear off and I was beginning to feel the sharp stinging of needle-like pain emanating from my self-inflicted wounds. It was still night-time, and I could hear the muffled sound of voices in the corridor. My mind was clearing; it would soon be time to engage the escape plan, upload my final report to HQ then get the hell out of here. But things were more complicated than I'd initially anticipated. Plus, there was the baby to consider now. Too much stress was bad for the baby. The transplant had been deemed a success - a first for mankind. The advances in medical research and technology had been amazing. The Swiss were on the cutting edge with transplant technology and anti-rejection drugs, giving people like me the opportunity to experience the ultimate human experience - childbirth. And here I was, proudly pregnant with Gerald's baby. What a miracle! There was no denying it - the ultrasounds, the remarkable images, and finally in the past few months, the gentle movements of our child growing inside me. I began to feel it too - a small kick, an elbow, the baby turning that made you feel delight and nausea all at the same time. Pregnancy was everything I dreamed it would be.

Once the new womb had been accepted and the body healed, losing my penis was a natural next step. If I was gonna have a baby then I wanted - no needed, to do it as a real woman. They fashioned my foreskin into a realistic labia. Nerves, blood vessels, veins and connective tissue were sown together. Cosmetically, it was quite simple; most of it was on the inside. But there was a real sensation now too, I could feel it all. To my delight, I could reach orgasm. But then again, sex has always been as much about the brain as the sexual organs themselves. I had experienced these intense feelings before in my mind; I'd practiced for that moment. My brain was already wired in anticipation of the new hardware. But oh, to look at myself in the mirror. Indescribable joy. And there I was – finally, a complete woman.

The door opened to my room. I closed my eyes and feigned sleeping. I gave it a moment and then squinted a little to get a sly look. All I could make out was a figure in a white lab coat, moving around, ghost-like, at the foot of my bed. He picked up the clipboard and leafed through my pages of medical notes. I heard him clear his throat as if to speak but stopped - a change of mind. I heard a small scratching sound, the noise of pen moving over paper. Then the figure moved closer to where I lay. I closed my eyes tightly, but I could feel his gaze on me, penetrating, analysing me. Then I heard my name –

'Yvonne.'

I opened my eyes and found myself looking up into his. Familiar eyes. Loving eyes. Just as quickly a hand came up and fingers gently pressed against my lips in a warning sign to remain quiet. Despite my shock and absolute wave of mixed emotions, my spy instincts kicked in. I sucked back on my feelings, remained quiet and still. He held a note up for me to read.

'Don't say a word. I've come to get you out –
Gerald x.'

'You seem to be very upset today, Yvonne?'

'Where is Gerald? What have you done with him?'

'We haven't done anything with anyone. Who is Gerald?'

'You know exactly who he is.'

Doctor Ross scribbled some notes onto his pad of paper and continued.

'Yvonne, we can't help you unless we are open and honest with each other.'

'Then why are you lying to me?'

'We're not lying to you, Yvonne. We are trying to help you get well again.'

'Lying bastards.'

'Do you want to talk about Gerald? Is he your boyfriend?'

'You know who he is. He was here. I saw him with my own eyes.'

'Yvonne, I can assure you there is no one here called Gerald. Why don't we talk about what he means to you?'

'And what about my baby? What have you bastards done with my baby?!'

The doctor scribbled some more notes and looked over at his colleague.

'You know Yvonne, it's not easy giving birth to your feelings, but perhaps we should take a break. You seem very upset today. Why don't we continue this tomorrow? I think you could use some rest', he said, glancing at the bandages on my arm. He nodded to his colleague and a nurse arrived with a hypodermic syringe and needle.

The lithium and midazolam effects were almost immediate. I fell into another deep drug-induced sleep but when I awoke, I only had one thing on my mind - find Gerald and get the hell out. Gerald had explained how he was completely undercover now, a top-level alpha mission which required the complete erasure of his identity. Hence, the faking of his own death - all staged and orchestrated by MI6. He knew how upsetting that would be for me, but still he hadn't been able to say anything at the time. I saw deep regret in his eyes though. Bless him.

I put his hand on my stomach to feel our growing child. He had no idea - until now. He kept his composure, but I could see the excitement and delight in his face. I had to fight back the tears, the joy of seeing him once again, sharing the news of our child - it's impossible to describe the avalanche of feelings. He'd be such a great father for our child. I just knew it. I felt such admiration for him.

Gerald straightened himself up, snapped back into spy focus again. But I could see by his name tag that Gerald didn't exist anymore. That identity had been erased. I read the new name: Dr. Carl Luger. Carl? I would have to get used to that.

Our interaction was short. Hurried. Gerald scribbled another note which read, 'hang in there, babe, back tomorrow. BTW congrats to us!' Then he acted the part of doctor. Initialled the charts, put them back at the end of the bed. With a final loving squeeze of my hand, he slid back into the shadows of the night. Back undercover. I clutched his note tightly to my chest.

'Congrats to us!' I wanted to cry so bad it hurt.

And that was the last time I ever saw him. Our last rendezvous. Reunited, so fleetingly, and then lost to each other again. In the morning a new doctor made the rounds. A cold-blooded woman – Dr. Frost. The irony, of which, wasn't lost on me. There was more probing, more checking of vital signs, more psychotic drugs prescribed to keep me under control. I knew what they were doing. They were just playing with me.

I knew then that Gerald had been caught. I had an intuition about these things - a woman's sense. He'd broken his cover, blown it completely. They knew. Damn it, Gerald - you fool, you! But isn't that how love is?

Doesn't it make us all do impetuous things sometimes? But how could I live with that? Losing him twice? He was probably being tortured somewhere. He wouldn't break though; he was too strong for that. They didn't know him the way I did.

I'm not sure how long I was knocked out - does it really matter? They had performed a caesarean section, stolen my baby away. They had it in an incubator somewhere, keeping the premature thing alive to use as leverage against me. I couldn't erase that awful image from my mind. The poor little helpless thing, motherless and abandoned, kept alive by devises and tubes. No human touch, no mother's breast to comfort it, no warmth, no love. What gave them the right? It belonged to me. It was my baby, my future.

Something welled up inside of me, an anger, a hatred, a mother's protective instinct. A feeling so primordial I could taste it. My womb - empty, abused, desecrated. Another scar, an intrusion, a cut so deep I don't think it will ever heal. I screamed at the wall, 'you scum-sucking bastards!'

I knew this wasn't gonna end well. You have a sense when it's game over don't you? I knew what had to be done. This is what every soldier is trained for and prepared to do when the eventuality comes. There can be no debate. The training is explicit. I was prepared.

Dr. Ross re-read the report. It was now ready for his sign-off. He had chaired the meeting. In attendance were Dr. Luger, Dr. Frost, Matron and Head of Security. There was a solemnity to the proceedings as there always is in these sorts of circumstances. It doesn't matter how long you've worked in mental health; these things are always unsettling and cast a long shadow. The inevitable root-cause analysis to unearth future recommendations. Dr. Ross still had his summary to write - the causative and preventative actions. Try to make damn sure it never happens again. Then there was the emotional fallout. Carl had taken it hard. Personal. He was the last one to examine Daniel. The young man had become fixated on him, but surely, he wouldn't have let down his guard? Carl would have known to keep a safe emotional distance from the patient - that's textbook doctor-patient. Dr. Ross adjusted his glasses and read on.

The psychiatric analysis: a twenty-five-year-old with paranoid schizophrenia. A young soldier back from a tour of duty in Afghanistan. Post-traumatic stress disorder. There it was in black and white. So obvious. Dr. Ross shook his head.

'Carl should have flagged this. Clearly one very troubled young man.' The coroner's report listed the actual death as 'multiple lacerations to the abdomen'. The toxicology report cited fatal levels of lithium found in the patient's bloodstream. Dr. Ross tried to take it all in.

'How could we have messed this up?'

Daniel had been found by a nurse making the early morning rounds. It was a grisly, alarming sight. She was already signed off on stress leave. The body contained multiple stab wounds, mostly to the stomach, but also across the arms and face. On the night table they discovered a most disturbing thing - a penis hacked off from the body. There would need to be an inquest now, a full investigation. Dr. Ross sighed deeply, thinking, 'Carl will be under the microscope on this one.'

He took a deep breath and picked up his pen.

'Well Carl', he said out loud echoing Carl's own words, 'looks like tomorrow we can die another day'. Then, Dr. Ross put pen to paper and began the onerous task of finishing his report

Luck

Serendipity. Synchronicity. Fate. Things that are just meant to be. Do you ever have feelings like that? That events are unfolding as they should before your very eyes? That somehow you just met that someone you were supposed to meet, just when it was right to meet them, and they turned out to be the one. Do you ever wonder why things happen as they do? Things like losing your job, feeling absolutely devastated, only to find something else, something better, unexpectedly showing up in its place. Nothing you would ever have planned for yourself, but now seems like a perfect fit for you. As one door closes another opens. Do you ever feel that life knows you better than you know yourself? That the road ahead is somehow prescribed beforehand by some hand of fate? Or what about those 'ah-ha' moments, where insight so clear and bright seems to hit you like a bolt of lightning.

That big idea. Pure unadulterated inspiration. Some might say, divine intervention. Yeah, I've felt like that.

I wouldn't say I wrote it, although obviously I did, but it felt more like it wrote itself, if that makes sense? It's one of those almost indescribable times when a writer feels like they are just hanging onto the tail of something bigger than themselves, being taken for a ride.
Inspiration. Pure and simple. You just know when you are in that zone. Any artist will tell you the same thing. I mean even Keith Richards describes it like that.

'I'm just a fucking antenna man' he says, 'I just stick my finger up into the ethos and grab a hold of a song.'

But that's exactly how I came to write *Supermodel - the musical*. Fifteen incredible songs pulled down out of the ethos. The seed of an idea that grew into a serendipitous flowering tree - nah, a whole forest of trees! It was magical, spiritual.

Supermodel - the musical is a story about the rise and fall of a near perfect specimen of womanhood. A reluctant, yet super, supermodel. Born into a rare Amazonian tribe, Zdu L (pronounced zoo-doo-el), was raised along the banks of an Amazon estuary, sequestered from the outside world until she was fifteen, when an American adventurer who just happened to be a fashion designer by trade, discovered her, brought her to London, taught her to speak the native tongue, mentored, groomed and then catapulted her onto the international stage of fashion, catwalks and designer labels. The entire world goes mad for her. She is exotic. Different. Beyond beautiful - if such a thing exists? A breath of fashionista fresh air. She has near-perfect bone structure. Long slender panther-like limbs. And God, that perfect skin. Unblemished, it literally shines like black glass. She is a child-god, a rare jungle orchid, an undiscovered gem that the world was waiting to *cherish* and *adore*. In fact, those are the words I coined to market her soon to be mega-successful perfume lines - *Cherish Zdu* & *Adore L.*

Although that's not in the script, I only came up with those for the purpose of the backstory, to flesh out the characters and storyline. It's something all writers do. All part of the development process. No, her rise to the top was meteoric. Swift and certain. How could it be, otherwise, everything was meant to be. Her management team made sure of the rest. Finding the Hope Diamond is one thing, making sure it sells, is another. And we all know how the wheels of commerce love to turn when the hottest young thing is at the bow of the ship - witness the Justin Biebers of the world. But, after making it in the fickle world of fashion, Zdu L finds a certain malcontent with her new celebrity status. Let's face it, it's hollow. A world that only values superficial things. The famous and beautiful. The beautifully famous. She becomes conflicted. Unravelling herself, however, from the machinations of the fashion industry is easier said than done. You don't just walk away from a six-figure career. Or do you? That would be what gave my story its twist, and every good story has to have one of those.

The fisherman is out in his boat. The Indian Ocean is calm today. The sun is setting red against an azure sky. The boat gently rocks back and forth as he pulls in his final net. Today's catch has been small. Just a few fish. But there is always tomorrow. Fishing is all he knows. He opens a small paper package prepared for him by his wife. She makes him the same supper every day. Bread, a simple stew, tea. He soaks the bread in the tea and takes a mouthful of stew. Within ten minutes the man is dead. The boat drifts listlessly with the tide, slowly making its way towards the shore. It will be two days before the man will be pulled from the water. The local medic will find a small chicken bone lodged in his throat.

OK, so that was the overall premise of *Supermodel – the musical*. The basic story. An unblemished innocent dropped into the gaping mouth of a ravenous flavour-of-the-week industry. But honing that into an engaging story worthy of a West End production was going to take perspiration as well as inspiration. But that's where my craft would come in. I had the songs, now I just needed the script. Shaping and honing the libretto was going to take some ingenuity, some gestative thought. But I just knew that what I was onto was going to be massive, a sure-fire blockbuster. The songs alone were amazing and the opportunity for costuming was a marketing wet dream. Who wouldn't want a piece of that? The major designer houses would be clawing at each other just to get their product placement. Givenchy, Klein, Prada. I could hear the sweet ring of the cash register now, the supersize-me royalty cheques. But this wasn't just going to be about the money. As sure as this thing had commercial appeal, I also wanted to make sure it had integrity. Depth. I wanted to create a great piece of art. I know what you're probably thinking - a musical? A great piece of art? But that was the challenge. I had studied theatre at Uni. Read all the classics. I was familiar with Chekhov, Ibsen and Strindberg. I knew how to make themes resonate more deeply. I understood the nuances of characterisations, the plot points, the rising action, the falling action, the crisis, the climax and the dénouement. *Supermodel – the musical* had to be worthy. Commercial yes, but endowed with rich theatrical overtones and allusions. There was a well-worn path to that end. The biggest playwright in the history of the world. Shakespeare.

A man sits in his bathrobe drinking a coffee, smoking a cigarette. It's his second of the day. He looks dishevelled. Depressed. Hungover. He is slumped on the sofa watching mindless morning television. This is the time he would have normally been making his way to work like all the other drones. But this day is different. On Friday he was called into the office. Chapter nine of the management handbook says you should always fire staff on a Friday. The conversation was short and to the point. They took his keys, his laptop, his swipe card and gave him a standard issue cardboard box with instructions to clear out his desk. Security escorted him to the front door. He had worked there for twelve years. The man looks up through bleary eyes at the images flashing across the TV screen. A plane flies into an office tower - the one the man used to work in - and explodes.

So, what does Shakespeare have to do with supermodels? Lemme explain. There is a great epic simile in Milton's *Paradise Lost* when Satan spies Eve for the first time in the Garden of Eden. He is so smitten by her beauty, her innocence, that for a brief moment he almost forgets his evil plan to bring about the downfall of mankind. I love that image of Satan falling in love with Eve. I remember writing an essay on this in Lit class at Uni. I somehow made the connection between Milton's Satan and Shakespeare's character, Angelo, from *Measure for Measure*. In the play Angelo falls in love with Isabella - another Eve-like character, who pleads with Angelo to save her brother's life. Angelo agrees to spare him on one condition: if she sleeps with him. This is pure serpent-tempting-the-innocent-beauty-in-the-Garden-of-Eden stuff. *Measure for Measure* is the only Shakespeare play to have overt Biblical references; the title itself refers to Jesus' *Sermon on the Mount*.

But ya gotta love the Bard; he could write the highest noble poetry, reflect the grandest Biblical ideals and also write the basest, audience-pleasing lusty story lines. These days he'd probably be cranking out racy crime dramas for American TV. *Measure* has it all in spades. I'm surprised it hasn't been made into a mini-series yet. So, riffing on his Biblical theme, Shakespeare used the name Angelo to allude to the fallen 'Angel', Satan, get it? Shakespeare - such a clever bastard.

Hang in there; I'm just about to make the connection to my play. Around this time, I'd begun sketching out my script and I found myself grappling with names for my own characters. I mean there is only so long you can call them 'female protagonist' and 'male antagonist'. Then it hit me. Why not use Shakespearean names for the characters I was creating? I mean you can't exactly give the movers and shakers of the fashion world ordinary names, can you? Meet the next great superstar of the runway - Jane? Just doesn't work. No offence to all the Janes out there but supermodels definitely need names that are a little meatier. Names that resonate. Shakespearean names! Well, if you're gonna steal, steal from the best, right? Something that would give it a classical flavour as well. So, I tried it out; my evil conniving agent character became 'Angelo' to allude to his more Satanic characteristics, Zdu L's best friend and photographer became Isabella, and her hairdresser became Claudio, all names borrowed from *Measure for Measure*. I thought they worked a charm.

Once I had the names in place I had another 'a-ha' moment - why not borrow a little bit of Shakespeare's love story and drop it into my play? Complete the allusion, tip of the hat to the master. You always need a good love story to spice things up. No need to reinvent the theatrical wheel. After all Shakespeare wasn't above borrowing, himself, from time to time. So, I created a love triangle between three of my characters: the evil Angelo, the innocent Isabella and luckless Claudio just like in

Measure for Measure. Now I had the final piece of my puzzle. A story set in the modern world of fashion and celebrity that had Shakespearean overtones and themes - the depth and resonance I was looking for. All the ingredients for success were present: a classic love story, hip modern songs, commercial costuming and appeal, and a transcendent ending. The critics would get it. The audiences would love it. Serendipity in action!

Script and songs finished, the next part of the process –get the industry boys to bite.

Abul watched Sajida and Nikesh from a distance. It had been a good day, a hard day, another day closer to their goal of reaching the temple at Nagarkot. Supper had been simple but satisfying - dried fruit, rice and tea. The sunset was glorious, the sky streaked with the most magnificent reds and golden bronze colours. Sajida could see the river down below, playfully dancing over the rocks as it made its way to the Indian plains. A mountain peacock, resplendent in full feathered beauty was foraging for food further down in the gorge. A good omen. Sajida stepped a little closer to the edge to behold its beauty and lost her footing. Abul looked up just in time to see his wife and Nikesh disappear before his very eyes, the crumbling earth giving way and swallowing them whole.

First, I needed to workshop the play, figure out the pacing, connect the dots, and make sure everything flowed. I hired a director and we set to work on figuring out a suitable schedule. There was some disagreement, or one could say, controversy, over the play's ending - the demise of Zdu L, but I knew that the story had to have a bona-fide crisis. A point where the protagonist must face up to some big deciding moment. This would happen in Act Two. I'll admit this was a bit of a sticky wicket, but a writer has to know when to stick to their guns. The idea came to me like another lightning bolt, so I knew I had to trust my instincts. Trusting my intuition was something I was becoming accustomed to. Learning how to stay in the zone. Ride the serendipitous stallion.

It was actually on a routine visit to my GP where I got the idea. I was sitting reading a magazine in the waiting room and there it was - an article about a new super drug just hitting the market called Xtraloss. A drug first developed for treating diabetes. Well, nothing so special about that, but it was how it worked that caught my attention. The drug inhibits the body's uptake of glucose. So, in laymen's terms - you can eat whatever you like, and the body simply disposes of it all. Eat what you want and stay thin? It was a no-brainer that a drug like that was bound to be abused by anyone with an eating disorder, dieters, and of course anyone whose job it is to look unrealistically thin. Geez, does a supermodel come to mind? Every story needs some sort of climax the audience would never expect, and I knew I'd just found mine.

A man steps out into the evening throng. There is a festive feeling in the night air. Many people mill about, chatting and smoking strong cigarettes. The man goes into a shop and buys a bottle of wine, a baguette, a small pot of cheese. As he leaves he passes a dark-skinned man wearing a New York Yankees baseball hat and carrying a backpack. They bump into each other. A momentary connection. The man walks back into the evening air and turns towards his home, a small second floor maisonette two blocks from this ordinary Parisian Plaza. His wife will be happy to see him. As he rounds the corner a terrorist bomb explodes destroying the shop and everyone in it. Nine people are killed.

Let me extrapolate. You see as everybody knows there comes a time when the tide will surely turn. How can it not? Everyone is apt to age, the best years slowly slipping away from you. Even pampered models can't avoid the inevitable. The only things we know for sure are death, taxes, and wrinkles. But when you are at the top of the game in an industry that only values perfection, the maintenance of your success becomes an institution. Agents, lawyers, managers, assistants, photographers, PR people, hangers-on of all kinds, everyone depending on you for their livelihoods. Wanting and needing your success to continue. The pressure to remain on top of the heap is enormous. Zdu L is different though - she sees through the facade. But she's between a rock and a hard place. In one sense she has grown accustomed to the life she has now – the limousines, parties, glitz and glamour - but another part of her longs for a time when life was simpler - back home in her Amazon village. This is the real emotional juice, the inner conflict of my protagonist, what drives her, what gives her motivation to act, and why the audience should care about what happens to her. I wrote a lovely poignant scene where Zdu L stands in front of the mirror one morning, questioning her own motives and beliefs. It's a transcendent moment. The emotional crisis. She has the world at her feet, anything and everything she wants is hers for the taking. She graces the cover of every magazine, is the toast of the town, is fawned over, celebrated, and worshipped. But is she really happy? Or was she happier weaving baskets in her mud hut? She can support her entire village now with her supermodel earnings. There is a scene in the second act where she sends money home and saves her entire village from smallpox - but I'm getting ahead of myself. In this scene she sings a tender ballad, *Top of the Heap*, to her mirrored image, an ode to a simpler life, a time before she was shackled to her fame.

What is it that I want
what is it that I seek
To be loved, to be famous
to be top of the heap
Am I glad for who I am
so elegant and chic
But was I happier before
I was top of the heap

Chloe got out her phone. There was something about Steve she liked. He was sort of cute and told her he was a writer. That definitely made him cool. She began adding his details into her phone when he abruptly revealed his wariness of the digital world. He was analogue all the way he said. Chloe shook her head, not understanding the translation of the word. 'Analogue. Old school' said Steve, 'here let me show you how we do things at Crazy Joe's'. Steve pulled out the only piece of paper he could drunkenly find in his wallet, wrote down his number, and handed the lotto ticket to the captivated Belgian girl.

OK, so now we had a little dramatic tension. More people have a stake in Zdu L than even she imagined. My protagonist is confused, conflicted, in crisis. Bring on the rising action of Act Two. Angelo has a proposal and makes her an offer she can't refuse. This will be the event of the year. There would be no retirement allowed for this supermodel, not while she could still command gazillions for pouting those luscious lips or strutting that million-dollar arse. But then one day things begin to change - she steps on the scales for the routine weigh-in and sees she's gained three pounds. Three pounds! Nothing to you or me, but everything to a model. The beginning of the end. I wrote a song called *Just Three Little Pounds,* an R&B number, in my humble opinion, destined to be a hit on and off the West End stage. Zdu L realises that if she wants to stay in the game she's going to have to find a way to stay thin. But she also realises this could be her way out. Get off the treadmill. Retire. The dramatic tension mounts.

Just three little pounds is all it takes
To make it or break it
do I love it or hate it
Should I stay in the game
do I like how that sounds
To be thin or be fat
just three little pounds

Another time for self-reflection, digging deep into her own psyche. The music was emotional, stirring; I knew there wouldn't be a dry eye in the house. But there is no rest for the wicked, she has the agents and managers negotiating terms and cutting deals, pushing her for one more cover shoot, one more traipse down the catwalk, one more chance to bankroll their retirement villas. And just like in the Garden of Eden Angelo tempts her with the forbidden fruit. OK, in this case it's the new wonder drug - Xtraloss. Something that can help her stay in the game. Only thing is, while it does work a charm, it comes with some pretty serious side effects. But Angelo doesn't give a shit about her wellbeing; he just wants that one more shot at the gold ring, the big prize money. He will work his evil charms to get her onto the catwalk one more time. So, I mentioned earlier there was a controversial twist? Well, this is it. The drug's side effects: uncontrollable flatulence and diarrhoea.

Sharon is a single mom, a young black woman living in Hackney, struggling to make ends meet. Every day she drops off two-year-old Sonia at a neighbour's flat. She doesn't like or trust the woman, but she has no choice. Every day she takes the tube further east and walks the final few blocks to the chain store where she works as a cashier. Every day she comes home to a freezing cold flat turns on the radio and sings to her daughter while she makes their tea. Beans. Sardines. White bread toasted. Whatever she has at hand. Affordable and quick. After supper she puts Sonia to bed and watches her sleep for a minute or two. Tonight, Sharon is tired, always tired. She opens the letter that arrived earlier that day. It is from the local college. She has been accepted into their business programme on a full scholarship. The letter explained how the scholarship will cover all her tuition expenses and the college has promised her a place for Sonia in its day-care.

I thought it was hilarious, and just what the show needed: uncontrollable flatulence and diarrhoea coming from the most expensive and revered arse in the world? Sheer comic relief. Shakespeare would have used a 'fool'; I used the almighty 'fart'. Picture this: in front of the world's press and a celebrity-filled audience Zdu L struts the catwalk for the biggest fee she's ever received. Her grand finale. Everyone who is anyone is there, flashbulbs are popping - this is the event of the year. Angelo has everything riding on this show and is pushing her to produce. He gives her a bottle of the magic pills and she defiantly takes a handful in front of him. Then she hits the catwalk, slinking along with long glamorous strides as the audience starts to chant her name. The side effects of the drug start to kick-in halfway down the runway and she unexpectedly lets one rip. She momentarily loses her composure but somehow makes it down to the end. But all the way there is one after another of gaseous blasts, emitting louder and more frequently from her wondrous derriere. At first the audience doesn't know what to do. But eventually the hushed titters turn into nervous giggles, then gales of laughter. She soldiers on but when she makes her classic twirl at the end she suddenly, and uncontrollably, let's fly with one final glorious almighty fart and shits herself on the spot. The place goes silent. She stands mortified in full model pose, in a pool of her own excrement. A few shrieks of disgust. Then the place erupts in hysterics. The show is a shambles. By tomorrow her career will be in ruins. The press will have a heyday. I knew this would be the turning point that every great show needs.

A mother steps lightly along her terraced house hallway. She hears the familiar metallic flap flap of the post being delivered. She picks up the letters strewn across her faded hall carpet. She hopes one is from her son.
Sunshine streams through the front window. She pauses for a moment and turns the letters over in her hands. There is one marked 'from her Majesty's service'. She takes them to the sitting room and pours a cup of tea. She tentatively opens the important letter first and holds it up to the light to read. She drops her cup onto the floor and lifts her shaking hand up to cover her mouth as muffled sobs form in her throat. In a far-off land a squadron of

British soldiers lay in the long dry desert grass. They watch the bombs explode in the distance. A few days earlier they lost three soldiers to enemy snipers.

Zdu L spends a night out with a girlfriend, getting drunk and trying to blot out the unfortunate events of the past twenty-four hours. This is her dark night of the soul. Her modelling career is in tatters and all she can do now is to stare into the black hole of washed-up celebrity status. Once top of the heap, the toast of the fashion world, now no one wants to know about her anymore. She's an embarrassment. She doesn't realise it yet, but this could actually be a blessing in disguise. Her agent has stopped returning her calls, the designer labels have dropped her and Angelo appears with the latest 'hot new thing' on his arm and proceeds to tear up his contract in front of her. Even the public has turned against her. The tabloids have a heyday. The incident is on the cover of every paper, magazine, and online blog known to mankind. *'Top model struts the crap-walk for the very last time!'*

And how the public loves a good scandal. We've seen it before. Down and out celebs. Amy Winehouse in rehab. The wanton drugs and boozing. Fist fights with her boyfriend. Shocking yet scintillating. Or Britney flashing her muff for the paparazzi after a drugged-out cat fight in a Hollywood nightclub. Tragic celebrities? Titillating Monday morning train fodder. The long hard fall from grace. Some might say, comeuppance. You made your celebrity bed, so lie in it. But people do love the misery of others. *Schadenfreude* the Germans call it - 'finding joy in someone else's misfortune'. Trust the Germans in all their efficiency to have one perfectly expressive word that sums up such a complex human condition.

Schadenfreude. The Germans are masters in the suffering game and can define it with clinical precision. Why do you think reality TV shows are so successful - to find and crown a new singing idol? Not a chance. The world is not wanting for another boy band. The real drama is in watching all those hopefuls get close to their dreams just to have a panel of overpaid celebrity tossers shatter them on live TV. The dreams of making it, so close, yet so far out of reach. C'mon, we all love Simon Cowell the best. He shoots from the hip and aims to kill. Saturday night it's all stars in their eyes but come Monday morning, it's back to stacking shelves at Tesco. Reality indeed. Zdu L finds herself a disgraced, washed-up supermodel. A victim of the fame game. Her career flushed down the tubes, ironically, in one big shitty mess.

   Schadenfreude. You bet.

The stripper got the Bible seller some more tea. She was a fallen woman, a sinner. It was clear what had to be done. While she was gone, he fingered the sharp blade he held in his jacket pocket. One meticulous cut is all it would take. There was a knock on the door. The Bible seller watched her as she glided across to answer it. It was another man. The Bible seller began to methodically pack up his samples and pamphlets. There would be another time, another chance to carry out God's will.

But I digress again. Zdu L wakes up from her dark night of the soul to an epiphany. A guardian angel, who looks strikingly like Kate Moss, arrives to show her a place where she can find true happiness. After all I didn't want to have this be a downer, a tragedy. No, hit musicals need to have uplifting, feel-good endings. Something to cheer for. A rousing finale to sell all those T-shirts, CDs and souvenir programmes. Well, they aren't gonna sell themselves. After her epiphany Zdu L rejects her celebrity life, gives the symbolic finger to Angelo and decides to return to her birthplace to rejoin the womenfolk of her village.

The dénouement.

The final scene is set at daybreak in her jungle village. One by one the Amazonian women make their way, baskets perched on heads, down to the river to begin the daily task of washing clothes. As the sun comes up, a glorious orb of life-giving light, drums start to beat in the distance. A rhythmic pulse begins as the song, *Wash Away Tomorrow's Cares* starts with a single woman's lament. The song grows as one by one the others join in. Voices rise up, first in unison then in harmony. The song, an ancient hymn handed down from generation to generation is about the simple truths in life, the everyday things that can bring joy to the heart. Zdu L is embraced back into the fold, takes up a washing basket and is soon working arm in arm with the others. As great colourful swaths of hand-woven fabric are hung out to dry in the morning sunshine, a glorious rainbow is created symbolising unity and love. The entire cast gathers on the stage. This is the big finale. By the end the song becomes a full-blown hand-clapping gospel sing-out with all the animals of the jungle coming to join in as well. Down they come, two by two, like Noah's Ark. Monkeys, zebras, crocodiles, and colourful parrots, all come down to the water's edge, entranced by the beautiful soul-stirring music. The costumes for this would be fantastic - imagine all the exotic creatures great and small joining the villagers, singing harmoniously about peace and joy on earth. Well, OK, I did rip that last part off of the *Lion King*, but what can I say - it looked great, and it worked amazingly well as an ending for the show.

It's 1959 and two expectant mothers sit and catch up over a coke and some chips in a local Wimpy Bar. They excitedly chat about the details of each other's pregnancy. The one who suffered extreme morning sickness is feeling much better now, thanks to a new wonder drug. The other mother hardly felt sick at all which, and as old wives' tales would have it, probably meant it would be a girl. Indeed, in six months, she would give birth to a perfect healthy daughter. The other's child would arrive shortly after missing both arms. It won't be until 1962 that the drug called thalidomide would be banned for use in pregnant women.

So that was it. The inspiration, the serendipity, the Shakespearean overtones, the songs and music, the beautiful costumes, all the ingredients that made up my musical. It was my ticket to the big time. But getting it onto the stage was gonna be no easy feat. Getting anything through the proverbial entertainment door and into the hands of a hot producer is an exhausting and almost undoable process. How do I know this? Before I wrote *Supermodel,* I had already shopped a couple of film scripts in Hollywood and let me tell you, LA is one hard nut to crack. It's a veritable locked-down fortress. Armed guards at all the studios. Checkpoint Charlie's at every parking lot. Gatekeepers everywhere you go keeping the wanna-be's outta Mr. Big's diary and limiting the access to Mr. Important Is speed dial. People sleeping on the sidewalks just to be in the vicinity of stardom, hoping for a chance to pitch their special project. Meanwhile, next door million dollar deals are going down in trendy Beverly Hills bistros. The beautiful people grazing themselves on organic Black Sea sushi, tuna tartare, pea-shoot caviar or whatever the hip food of the day is, while contracts are negotiated and percentages are sliced and diced. It's a surreal world, a most bizarre paradox. LA is a mythic paradise alright, full of the hopes and dreams of every kid that grew up and wanted to become an actor, a recognisable face in some movie or TV show. Every creative writing hack who packed up their typewriter, hitched a ride to California and dreamed of making their fortune writing the next Hollywood blockbuster. In Los Angeles every waiter is an actor in-waiting, every busboy is a director, and every line-cook has a script ready to pitch in their back pocket. Everyone rubbing up against the edge of stardom, tempting it like fate. Praying that serendipity might cast its gold their way. Hollywood - the stuff that dreams are made of. But I've digressed again.

The two young women decided to leave the endless queue and get a drink in the pub next door. The Asian girl hated waiting and it was looking more and more like their dates had bailed on them. The Blind Beggar was only half full and had plenty of seats, not a common occurrence on a Friday night on Camden high street. They ordered drinks and began to figure out what Plan B would be. Across the room was an attractive young man. Attractive in a literal sense, this guy seemed magnetic, mesmerising. He introduced himself as Warrington. Without realising why, the two women soon found themselves guests at his table as he charmed them with his stories. As the evening unfolded it looked like Plan B would be nothing like they had thought.

To get my play seen I entered it into a competition for new 'emerging' playwrights. After every writer had submitting a synopsis and song samples from their shows, a group from the local playhouse gathered to sift through the dross. Naturally *Supermodel* rose to the top, made the cut. But it's not as if it had stiff competition. The other entries were full of misaligned hopes and false expectations - nothing that was in the same league as

Supermodel. Once the picks of the litter were decided, dates were booked, rehearsal rooms secured, and posters were created to advertise the four musicals that would compete against each other for a place in the final. Every show got thirty minutes before a paying audience to strut their stuff and wow the pundits. Then the audience and a panel of illustrious theatrical veterans would cast their votes and the favourites would make their way to the final round. We had one crack to pull it off.

On our night, the first performance was a play based on the travails of the Doukhobors. These Russian immigrants settled in the Canadian hinterlands in the 1950s and were avowed pacifists. Believing in the living spirit within each individual and in the transmigration of souls, they expressed opposition to civil authority by refusing to pay taxes and do military service. So, in return, the Canadian officials interned their children into camps, wrenched them right from the bosom of their families and homes. The Doukhobor protestors, or 'Sons of Freedom' as they coined themselves, would gather every week in front of the local government offices to protest. These peaceful gatherings were always done stark naked. Sound sexy? Not in the slightest. It wasn't sexy then and it certainly wasn't sexy in this musical. Unfortunately, their producer hired a group of middle-aged saggy-bottomed actors gotten on the cheap. Not a stitch of clothing in sight. It was hard to watch. Awkward. There were pale, flabby naked bodies everywhere. Couple that with the fact the playwright had gone to immense trouble to authentically replicate the traditional songs of the Doukhobor choirs. Have you ever heard a Doukhobor choir singing in protest? Let me tell you, I've never heard a more cheerless sound in all my life. So, *Sons of Freedom - the musical* had two serious problems: an almost completely tuneless drone of songs sung by a cast of unattractive naked actors. Doubly unpleasant.

By Tower Bridge, right under one of the parapets, sits a homeless man, blanket draped over his shoulders, paper cup down at his feet. His heroin buddies call him 'Rent'. Everyday Rent sits here. Counting on the gratitude of strangers. He rarely gets more than a couple of pounds of change in his cup. Today he has even less. It's a cold wintery day, the rain has been ceaseless. The grey gloom of another freezing evening is about to descend. He doesn't have enough to buy a hit to see him through the night. He picks up his plastic bag of worldly possessions, adjusts the dirty blanket on his shoulders and shuffles off towards the underpass. On the steps he spies a wallet. There is no one around. He picks it up. Inside it is flush with £20 notes. There is probably more than a couple thousand pounds in there. A windfall.

The next musical on the bill was a show with distinct feminist overtones titled *Seahorses*. The entire thing took place in the underwater world of a coral reef. I had no idea until I saw the show that the seahorse is the only species on earth where the male becomes pregnant and bears the young. You can google it yourself - it's a fact. I think the writer was trying to make some postmodern feminist point about true freedom for women. I think she was trying to illustrate that equality between the sexes would only come to pass once the male species did some of the grunt work and birthed the children. I mean really? I suppose in the world of the metaphor anything is possible, but this seemed like quite a stretch to me. But I guess everyone is entitled to their own creative misfirings. But other than the premise seeming a bit dodgy, I have to admit the costuming and staging looked fabulous. Lots of underwater montages of beautiful sea creatures living in a decidedly sensual world. The ballad by the transexual sea urchin being my favourite. The hermaphrodite lobsters were pretty cute too, and the duet of the two prostitute scallops was nothing short of marvellous. Come to think of it, most everything in the play had to do with the underwater sex lives of crustaceans and sea creatures. What that had to do with raising the profile of feminism is beyond me. Unfortunately, I didn't see the second act, as we were readying for our own performance, but it apparently featured a mutual masturbation scene by a humpback whale and a dolphin. *Seahorses* did receive a fair amount of the audience vote. Go figure.

The surgeon made a hard decision. He'd seen this sort of thing before, a cancer that had spread throughout the whole body. There would be no fixing, no curing, no saving a life this time around. The patient had perhaps six months to live. He gave the order with a solemnity he was used to - sew her up again and recommend to the family that the patient get their affairs in order. Sam sat out in the waiting lounge, nervous and worried, awaiting news of Lynn's procedure. He hadn't had a chance to tell her of his recent lay-off from work. About the financial black hole they were in. He really hoped there wouldn't be any more bad news today.

The final performance of the night was a musical remake of the film *Rain Man*. Its storyline and characters were lifted directly from the Oscar-winning screenplay of the same name. Needless to say, the judges sat up and took critical notice. The only thing new was the addition of some spotty songs. There was a little controversy over this - whether it should have even been allowed as an entry in an 'emerging musicals' competition. I mean the script was a direct lift and they had even cast a Dustin Hoffman look alike. Talk about stealing. Besides, I found the music to be rather pedestrian. OK, so that's being polite, the songs were more like hard little unhummable turds. Absolute shit! I mean one song was, in its entirety, based on the scene where an autistic character (sung by the Dustin Hoffman look alike) sings an endless series of seemingly random numbers. Just one after another. Let me see if I can hum a few bars for you – '8, 3, 5, 9, 1, 3, 1, 7, 6, 7. . .'get the picture? For three-and-a-half painful minutes. That's three-and-a-half minutes I'll never get back. Bloody mesmerising in its stupidity is how it sounded. The closest thing resembling a song you could actually sing was a number sung by a psychiatrist character, called 'Medication Medication', while several glassy-eyed actors pranced around the stage in strait jackets. Medicate me, I say. But I guess there is no accounting for the tastes of the theatrical cognoscenti because *Rain Man* got voted through to the final. I'm guessing mostly on the strength of its Oscar-winning script. Which probably sounds like sour grapes. But in reality, I couldn't find much else to praise.

The young man knew he had been reckless. He blamed the alcohol, the drugs, his insatiable desire to fuck and be fucked. For the past two years he'd cruised the leather bars, the bath houses, the gay discotheques. Anything that moved, he had sex with. He'd lost count of his conquests. He'd played the odds, and he knew it. Now he awaited the news. The phone rang. It was the clinic. The results were back. He was negative. Thank God. He breathed a sigh of relief, checked his look in the mirror, pulled on his leather trousers and readied himself for another night of clubbing.

So, that was that, four plays made it through to the final: *Rain Man*, *Supermodel*, *iTalk*, (an overtly ironic play about internet dating), and *She Said, She Said*, a romantic comedy involving the mishaps of a lesbian couple set on the Greek island of Lesbos. In an attempt to replicate the rash of successes by the popular jukebox musicals such as *Mama Mia*, and *We Will Rock You*. *She Said, She Said* borrowed from the song catalogue of Boney M for its soundtrack. Yes, the songs were tried, true and tested, but I found it hard to accept the premise that Rasputin was recast as some butch dyke. And for me the *Rivers of Babylon* will always conjure up Biblical images and not the notion of some tributary leading to an island of oral sex loving lesbians.

I'll spare you the hoary details of that finale evening expect to say that *She Said, She Said* sank like the Greek drachma, *iTalk* was more like *iWank,* and the illustrious judges couldn't find enough accolades to describe the depth and richness of *Rain Man - the Musical.* Go figure. And *Supermodel?* Needless to say, it failed to impress and had its opening and closing night all at once. My bon-a-fide hit song, *Just Three Little Pounds*, failed to bring the roof down, and the big finale fell flat.
Apparently, the percussionist we had hired to play the all-important jungle rhythms got the dates mixed up and simply never showed. *Rain Man* was hailed the winner and went on to win a development package with the local theatre company. I expect we'll be seeing it in the West End in a year or so being promoted mostly on its Oscar merits. So I was left to pack up the animal costumes, clean up the fake shit, and put *Supermodel – the Musical* back on the shelf. Serendipity? Well, to quote Mr. Shakespeare . . . 'Our remedies oft in ourselves do lie, which we ascribe to heaven: the fated sky'

Martin unpacked the last of his belongings, straightened his shirts and laid out his ties. He would iron everything later, now it was time to relax, put his feet up with a glass of wine. The drive to Montreal had been a long one. It was strange to be sharing a wardrobe and dresser with someone else again. His clothes, mixed up with another woman's. Someone other than his wife. But life goes on. It had been a hard but heartfelt decision. Cathy put her hand on his shoulder - a gesture of understanding and caring. Martin looked up and into her eyes. They were the same kind eyes he had met last summer in Paris on Le Pont de l'Archevêché.

Which all brings me to luck. We all know what that is. In an overt sense, it could simply mean something like winning the lottery. What are the chances that your numbers will come up? Well, I'm sure some mathematician has already calculated the odds of that one. Or what about meeting your soulmate. That perfect complement to yourself - your other half. A chance encounter with another human being, eyes meeting for the first time across a crowded room. A love story about to unfold. But only if you are in the right place at the right time. Luck?

Or how about missing your flight on that particular day. Perhaps it was the cross-town traffic that delayed you or maybe you overslept the alarm. Whatever. The reasons don't matter. Or do they? Reality is, you miss the flight only to watch the gory details on the 6 o'clock news of flight 587 going down in a fireball of flames. No survivors. Except you. Luck?

Think about this for a minute. What if everything is really all down to that one thing - luck. There is nothing else, no hand of God, no fate, nothing 'meant to be', no destiny. Nothing but luck. What if the entire universe was run on that premise? Evolution is really just luck. Things routinely reproducing until eventually there is a single mutation and the course of history changes all because of some lucky one-in-a-million event. The formation of the first big bang - just luck. The weather systems that bring us the perfect long hot summers providing us a magnificent bumper harvest. Luck. The hurricanes, storms, floods and other natural disasters that seemingly destroy at random. Just bad luck. Life as we know it - just one long series of seemingly disconnected yet continuous lucky or unlucky events. What if all those serendipitous moments are really just luck in disguise, the culmination of a random universe rolling its dice.

The woman lifts the hood of her car. It is a useless gesture. Staring down into an engine full of wires, gaskets and motor parts as if she would know what was wrong if it slapped her in the face. She calls for roadside assistance. The voice informs her the wait time will be between one to two hours. She is irritated but finds a coffee shop nearby. She buys a paper, skinny latte, and makes the best of things. A few miles away two men break a small pane of glass and gain entry to the apartment. They ransack the place, taking anything of value, anything they can sell. During the last burglary they stabbed a man to death when he arriving home unexpectedly, disturbing their activities. The woman's phone rings. It is the security company. There has been a break-in at her home.

So, what happened to *Supermodel - the musical* - the play that fate wrote?

Nothing.

It was never to be heard of again. Sure, it's a shame the world will never get to hear those brilliant songs. I'll never be presented with my very own Tony award for best new musical. My bank account won't fill up with massive royalty cheques. Unfortunately, the world is full of great art, artists, music, ideas, science, innovations, inventions, you name it, that never get to see the light of day. All just missing that important ingredient - luck.

There are painters as good as the great masters living humble lives, producing great art every day, that never get discovered. I've seen them. They work as waiters.

There are musicians and composers whose music never makes it past the local bar scene, or never becomes more than a scribble of black dots on the manuscript paper. It's criminal. They work as busboys.

There are writers and poets, writing stories and verse as imaginative and entertaining as any of the literary greats. It's likely they might have cooked your lunch today.

No, I licked my wounds, went back to my day job sweeping floors and cleaning office garbage cans and tried to make sense of the senselessness that is life. I still believe that *Supermodel* is great and could have been a massive hit. In the end, I guess, you just have to accept your lot in life. Or maybe your luck in life.

Out in the middle of the Pacific Ocean, deep beneath the surface, on the ocean bed, the Tectonic plates that join the two great continents start to shift. At first the movement is almost immeasurable, undetectable, but of great significance none-the-less. Its reverberations would be felt for miles around. A wave created by this tremor starts to grow and move in a singular direction. By the river estuary of an otherwise deserted shoreline a young mother gently puts down a woven basket while she attends to the daily chore of washing clothes. In the basket is her baby daughter. She is sleeping now, contented, oblivious to the world around her. She is a near-perfect child, her mother's pride and joy. The woman has named her Zdu L, after a great jungle plant whose seed pods contain many healing properties. The woman lifts her eyes to survey the horizon. It is dawn; the day is filled with beauty and promise. Her heart is full up with joy. She begins to hum a simple hymn, a song of thanks to the great spirits. In the distance, far from the eye's view, the tsunami gathers momentum as it makes its way towards the unsuspecting shoreline.

Cripples & Creeps

The girl couldn't be more than twelve at the most.
It's hard to tell really 'cause the disease stunts growth.
Another side effect.
A real cripple.
Everyday the world goes by her kitchen window.
And everyday she watches
the normal kids on their way to school.
Everyday she wishes she could be one of them.
Everyday she wishes for something else.
Everyday.

Oh, she has people who take care of her,
feed her, bathe her, talk to her.
Love her.
People who want to do good things
for those less fortunate.

Good people with good intentions.
Sometimes she feels the world is so fucking full
of good people with good intentions.
Everyone wanting to help make
her spastic life somehow better.
Sometimes people take for granted
the simple pleasures in life.
Pleasures like walking to school.
Wiping your own ass.
Making your own goddamn oatmeal.
Making your own choices.
Like killing yourself.

Then there's this other kid
see him every day.
A complete creep.
Fat. Stupid looking.
Glasses. Greasy hair.
Never smiles. No reason to.
No friends. A real teenage outcast.
Didn't choose to be this way.
Unlucky as a bad penny.
Kinda kid you just know, you can feel it
when you walk past him,
gonna snap one day like a rotten branch,
walk into school, pull out a gun,
and wipe away all that fuckin' sadness.
Happens everyday.

I sat watching these horses
just regular horses,
brown and all that, running free in a field.
The late evening sunshine shining
on their glossy muscular backs.
One of them had an erection.
A massive pink horse-cock protuberance.
Fascinatingly comical.
There was a cool edge to the early autumn air.
A spider's web of horse breath, dew covered,
hanging suspended in the descending shiver of night.

I remembered a story about my grandfather.
How he worked the land when he was a young man.
Life was simple then.
Just a man and his horse toiling
with the soil and weather.
Long hard days under an undiscriminating sun.
The mutual respect between man and beast.
An unspoken trust.
Then the contained sadness and stoic acceptance
of nature's ways when old Bessie grew crippled
and had to be put down.
A single bullet.
The unavoidable cycles of life and death.

The guy with no teeth and bad breath
broke my silent meditation.
'Sure tell 'em's male horses'
and he laughed that throaty, ashtray laugh.

I stared in silence as the walls around me closed in again.
The smoke of the bar burned my eyes
and the horses in the field drifted off into shadows.

I looked around the dim room at all the broken faces.
The broken lives.
A regular watering hole for all the lost hopes and dreams.
You see it all the time in bars.
The lowlifes. The lonely.
The alcoholics. The drifters.
The angry. The forgotten angels.
All together.
Alone.

Staring at their bleak lives through the bottom of a glass.
A draft beer and a pack of smokes.
Whining about their pitiful, shit-filled lives.
Crappy, dead-end jobs.
Welfare Wednesdays.
No luck, no hope, no choices.

Another round?
Oatmeal?
Choices.
People make them everyday.

Except for the cripples and creeps.

About the Author

Jude is a composer, musician, recording artist, and author. He has written and produced 20 albums of varied musical styles and genres with songs that include Americana, rock, pop, country, soul, gospel, blues, mariachi, Dixieland, and even a trilogy of spoken word & music albums. His songs have been licensed to numerous TV shows - *Baywatch*, *Cold Squad* and heard in feature films - *Return to Turtle Island*, *The Raffle* (with the soundtrack featuring Elton John and Dan Hill), and his first single, *Lifeline*, reached number 25 in the USA adult contemporary charts.

Between 2009 and 2012 Jude released the back-to-back critically acclaimed albums, *Circo de Teatro*, the sprawling double disc, *Outskirts of Eden*, and his most recent album, *Head Bone Gumbo*, all of which are distributed in the UK/Europe by Proper Records. In April 2011 both Circo and Eden received recognition at the BCIMA Awards winning Concept/Collaboration Album of the Year and Best Artwork/Graphics, respectively. All these albums have garnered rave reviews, receive radio airplay throughout Europe and North America, and have sparked comparisons to Tom Waits, Bob Dylan, and Lyle Lovett.

Jude has co-written two screenplay projects. *Drop Dead Scene* is about an imaginary LA rock band called Fetish and features an edgy 'soundtrack' album of original rock songs – *Neurotic Erotica*. Set in the post-plague future, *Slow Resurrection* follows the life of cowboy troubadour, Leland Frank and features the country soundtrack album *God's Big Radio* – a collection of traditional-sounding americana songs. This project evolved and toured as a multi-media theatrical production, featuring poetry, video, and live music.

In 2016 Jude released his first book of short stories – *Cripples & Creeps* and quickly followed this with a musical memoir – *Unspoken Heaven*. In 2019 he began work on his first novel, *Cybersoul*, which was originally conceived and written in the form of a stage musical.

The novels: *The Underwater Birds* and *A Writer's Prerogative* quickly followed and *Small Cruelties* is his second book of short stories. He lives with his wife in beautiful Cumbria, England. For more information and to listen to his recordings please visit:
www.judedavison.co.uk

A Writer's Prerogative

Revenge - what lengths would someone go to get retribution for perceived betrayal and hurts?

Midnight, Manhattan, and famous reclusive author Carson Crowe, sips his Scotch, stubs out a cigarette, and emails his final book manuscript to his agent . . . then kills himself.

Carefully orchestrating things himself, a week later seven family and friends gather to hear the author's final wishes. Speaking through a pre-recorded video, Crowe reads excerpts from his own bestsellers, the fictional character depictions singling out each person individually and the wrongs they have done him.

Crowe's fascinatingly deceptive stories include two astronauts on a daring space mission; a duplicitous medieval abbot; Satan overseeing her debauched underworld; and a poetry-loving murderer on a prison break.

In turn, each at the gathering finds themselves the target of Crowe's artfully revengeful skewering. But two questions remain - who will inherit his fortune and what is the meaning behind the strange packages the author has gifted to everyone?

The Underwater Birds

For some, running away to join the circus is a dream, but for others it's a last chance for redemption and survival. Traverse the harsh American landscape from the 1930s to the 1960s along with
Ringmaster, Sam O'Reilly, and his self-proclaimed, 'Greatest Show on Earth'.

Behind the mesmerising display of big-top daring tricks, animals, and clowns, are the people. Meet One-Eyed Pete and the tattooed Madeleine, the Midway act 'Beauty & the Beast'; Lee and Kwan, the singing Siamese Twins; Madame O and her mysteriously telling tarot; and Dalvinder Singh, who charms his King Cobra nightly into submission. Each one with a backstory of pain, heartache and skeletons locked away.

In 1962, as Sam lies dying, his circus family pay homage. Revelations unravel, fate unearths a secret, and life takes a twist. For some, everything changes, but for most, the show must go on.

Cybersoul

As the world descends into chaos, a young cyborg tightens the noose around his neck. How could life spiral down into such a black hole? The cyborg terrorist revolutionaries attacking the clones; the riot police retaliating with public hangings; executions being streamed live across the entire sector; and true love failing. The new world order brings a class struggle, social unrest, and injustice where an interracial love has no hope to survive.

Watching over these proceedings is a trio of guardian angels, the Soul Sisters, who are there to remind us that everything and everyone are connected through the universal energy of love.

'Without love, you ain't nothing but a Cybersoul!'

Originally written as an allegorical stage musical, *Cybersoul* was inspired by the U.S. black civil rights movement and soul music of the 1960s. Here, the songs inform each chapter and add a lyrical poetry to the story.

small cruelties

Small Cruelties is an entertaining and, at times, poignant collection of short stories. Amongst them: a naïve couple accidentally stumble upon the brutality of a Mexican bull fight; a convicted murderer is made to practice his electric chair execution; a young man is propositioned by a husband-and-wife duo of swingers; a narcissistic film star writes his own obituary; and the accidental growing of a beard leads a man to unwittingly find himself the object of attraction by the sophisticates of the London fashion world.

Sometimes gritty, sometimes humorous, nostalgic or tender, the stories crisscross the globe from the back streets of Belfast to a prison in North Dakota, from a motel in Los Angeles to the undulating rivers and rolling countryside of Cumbria.

Exploring a gamut of themes and emotions the stories come together to chronicle the human experience and remind us of the uncertainty, fragility, joys and tribulations that make up our lives.

Uncertain Heaven
a musical memoir

From first picking up a guitar, to writing songs and discovering a connection to the universal source of creativity, Uncertain Heaven is a rock 'n roll memoir that tells the story of one man's creative path, a journey that becomes inextricably intertwined with a search for the meaning of our existence and mankind's relationship with God.

A story of record deals, songs heard by billions on syndicated television shows, the highs and lows of an indifferent music industry, the painful reality of playing 'music-by-the-yard' and the sheer joy of putting your finger up into the ethos and downloading a song - just like Keith Richards.

After years of following the muse wherever she leads, an existential crisis leads the author to peel back the mysteries of life itself, follow what surely seems meant to be, only to find himself standing on the precipice at his own potential demise.

Printed in Great Britain
by Amazon